Lessons From The Sauna

- the perils of online dating & more -

by

Michael Klerck

a vonPeter Publication
Copyright © 2016 :: Michael von Petersom Klerck

All rights reserved. No part of this publication may be reproduced, stored in a retrieval system or transmitted in any form or by any means – electronic or mechanical – without the prior written permission of the author.

ISBN-13: 978-9781530995455
ISBN-10: 1530995450

Other books by Michael Klerck

From Biltong
to Beef Jerky & Beyond – autobiographical travelogue

Where The Light Is – adult, literary novel

The Key To Tantalis – fantasy/adventure for graders

View these at **MichaelKlerck.com** for details of the books & links to online bookshops. Available in e-book format for devices as well as in paperback, shipped worldwide. Unfortunately, because of multiple tables this book is not available digitally, except in pdf format.

**This and other books are also all available
in paperback at major online bookstores, including
Amazon.com, Barnes and Noble, etc.**

ABOUT THE AUTHOR

Michael Klerck was born in 1955, in Cape Town, South Africa and soon went on to spend a significant part of his childhood on the infamous Robben Island where his parents met during the war. He began writing at an early age, and concentrated for some time on writing short stories, one of which was published by Stand Magazine, Newcastle. He qualified as a teacher at the then well-known Graaff-Reinet Teachers' College, and went on to gain a Bachelor of Arts degree through the University of South Africa where he read courses in Economics, Communication and Philosophy while majoring in Psychology and English. He spent six years teaching in the former homeland of KaNgwane near Swaziland and began lecturing in tertiary education in 1987 which saw him involved in a number of pilot teaching programmes.

He is the author of a number of textbooks for the college market, including one on Public Finance that has enjoyed one of the longest uninterrupted runs in the college market since first published in 1996.

He has also had various articles published by Men's Health, South Africa, and is the winner of the 2001 Mondi Paper Magazine Writer's Award for work in the same magazine.

He is the author of the novel **The Key To Tantalis**, a children's fantasy book, and an adult literary novel called **Where The Light Is**.

And his autobiographical travelogue, **From Biltong To Beef Jerky & Beyond.**

He lives in White Rock, near Vancouver, British Columbia.

ACKNOWLEDGEMENTS

- *so many* -

Cheryl, for all the edits, and the belief that I got it right this time - Jane, thanks for being the English professor that enthused - David, the only person who has read all my books and comes back for more - Carol, whose idea this was, after we met on the deck that day - Cathy, for saying you think I have found my niche - I think you are right.
To Trevor Webster and André Lemmer, for their abiding belief in me as a young student in their English class in the seventies.

Also Chris Bowling who, as my mentor and even when I wrote a novel that did not deserve to be read, he read it and encouraged me.
It saddens me to know he never got to see me published.
This one is for you, Chris.

~ *In memory of Drywer Du Toit, and others* ~

Contents:

1. Visiting Greenland 8
2. Women With Small Dogs 18
3. Taking A Peek 28
4. Three Kings From Afar 41
5. A Fit 56
6. When The Trains Roll By 76
7. Too Hot To Handle 107
8. Serving Papers 128
9. La Petite Mort 151
10. The Right Ingredient 175
11. The Screaming Of Those Lambs 197
12. When War Was Right 223
13. Finding My Angel 240

1
Visiting Greenland

Oom is not an easy word to pronounce.
Especially for the Dutch.
This is difficult to explain to most people because it is a Dutch word.
It is also very difficult explaining this to the Dutch themselves.
Whenever someone asks me why some people call me Oom, I have to give them an explanation, and then also say where the word comes from. And that people from Holland cannot pronounce it as it should be pronounced.
This sometimes leaves them feeling they should perhaps not have started a conversation with me.
With some people this is an advantage.
But with others, I feel the explanation could be a bit of a problem. So if I like someone, I leave out the Dutch portion of the explanation so as not to confuse them.

It is only because someone who went to my school started calling me *Oom*.

Not necessarily because I feel old, but because it is a title that younger people use for older men, and this friend is younger than me. It is also because when I moved to Canada, I started speaking more Afrikaans than when I lived in South Africa. That's another story, and I am not going to bore you with it right now.

This particular person from my school is ten years younger, and so when we became friends he called me Oom as a joke, but it stuck with me.

So I am Oom. The simple translation is *Uncle*.

And it is used just like Indian people use the word *Aunty*: out of respect for an older woman of standing in the community.

I am not a woman, but I think you know what I mean.

Although we have many people from India in South Africa, I first heard this title, *Aunty*, here in Canada. If you were born in North America you probably also pronounce this word differently, as in *Anty*.

But it should sound like this: *Onty*.

As I have said, in South Africa, there are many people from India who live in Durban, but very few in Cape Town. The only Indians I remember were the Osmans who seemed to own every convenience store, on the corner of almost every street. But apart from this family, most of them stayed in Durban where it is hot and there are more sharks. Although I don't want to digress too much at this point, the Indians in South Africa are mainly Hindus.

The people from India, in Canada, are all Sikhs.

They wear turbans.

Of course I am speaking about the men, and not the women. Although the women are also Sikhs.

The Hindus would never be seen dead in a turban. I think it is because they talk so fast and so much, it would fall off.

I remember going to Durban once; there I visited a shop. I was exhausted when I left, because when I came out onto the street I found I had products in my arms I had never seen before.

My wife, Emma, who was still alive then, said she would never go to India with me.

You can imagine my surprise when we arrived in British Columbia and I found that there was a whole city of people from India.

They are the Sikhs I was talking about. They are very different. A lot quieter and very hard working.

But beware. If you are not careful, you will end up with as many products in your arms, just with them looking silently at you.

They are very generous people. And when I visit their city which is called Surrey, and enter the sauna, there is always an *Aunty* who looks for a younger man after seeing me arrive, and just says one word: *respect*. And at least two younger men jump up and offer me a seat. I am often embarrassed by this, but I sit down anyway.

And when they discover where I come from originally, and I mention all the Indians in Durban, I get a funny look from them. I am now careful not to say much about Hindus.

Anyway, the point is that I get to sit down because

an *Onty* has made sure that one of her family shows respect. And I am always grateful, and often wonder whether it was the British that taught them this respectful way of doing things.

Or if it was the other way around.

Thank goodness I am not *Oompie*. But that is yet another explanation.

So, in Dutch, Oom is pronounced just as English-speaking people pronounce *ohm* which is the *resistance in a circuit transmitting a current of one ampere when subjected to a potential difference of one volt.*

Neither this definition nor the word itself has anything to do with my name, except that one woman did tell me once she thought I was electrifying.

Now if you pronounced Oom like this - *ohm* - no one in South Africa would understand you.

But in Holland, they will not understand you when you pronounce it the way it should be said.

Everybody talks about the *Dutch* in *Holland*. But there is no country called Holland, a Dutch person told me one day. He said we should be calling it *The Netherlands*. I realised that with such confusion about the name of their own country, it is no wonder they don't know how to pronounce *Oom* properly.

It should be pronounced like this: *Oo-wim*. This is the way we say it in Afrikaans; the proper way.

It occurred to me one day that I would hate for people to meet me in the street and shout, *hey, Ohm!*

Instead of, *hey Oo-wim!*

Many years ago I visited Holland as a student, and stayed with a family. They had a daughter who liked to engage with me at the dinner table every night. I used to speak a little Afrikaans to her and her mother, just as a tease. She loved this because deep inside her she could understand what I was saying, but on the surface she could not. I think it was like being able to smell the rain that splashes on the dry African soil, but at the same time not having it touch your skin.

It is strange.

I used to say "*Die ooo-wimm sit in die boo-wim.*" The uncle sits in the tree.

And she would bend over double with laughter, because in Dutch it should have been *De ohm zat in de bohm*.

This never sounded right to me.

Every night she would ask me what the *ohm* was doing. And I would tell her, and she would burst out laughing all over again. I even drew her a picture of an oom in a tree, and each night I made sure there was something different about him. One day I made his beard longer. She noticed and asked me why. I said because he had been in the tree for some days and could not trim it. She found this very funny.

I soon found out why they pronounced *oom* incorrectly.

One day I added a little stream below the tree. And some flowers next to the stream, because the Dutch love flowers. I cannot remember if they were specifically tulips, but nevertheless.

She looked at me and asked what it was at the bottom of the tree. I was a little insulted because to me it was obvious. But when I told her, she giggled with renewed delight.

And then I knew why they had it wrong with *oom*.

It was because they also had it wrong with *stroom*.

In Afrikaans stroom would be pronounced just like oom. One simply adds the *str-* in front of *oo-wim*. So my drawing would be: *Die oo-wim sit in die boo-wim, boo-er die stroo-wim.* The uncle sits in the tree, above the stream.

In fact it was Gord, my confidant in dating, who alerted me to the fact that *bo* could be pronounced as one would say *Boer* in English, or Luxembourgish.

Gord was born in Luxembourg. I didn't even know there was a language called Luxembourgish.

And they say *boer*, just like the Engelse would say it: *baw-er.*

It sounds like it rhymes with *abhor*.

This makes sense because the Engelse did abhor the Boers. Mostly because the Boers almost beat them.

But that is another story.

Of course in Dutch they had it all wrong, and when she had finished laughing at me, she said it like this: *de ohm zat in de bohm, boh-ve de strohm.*

I smiled, even though the pronunciation was entirely wrong.

Perhaps, I thought, the Dutch would one day come back to Cape Town, and then learn to say it correctly.

When the oom in the tree had grown a long beard, and we were both a little tired of him, I decided to do something else.

I decided to share a poem.

I was sensitive enough not to simply blurt it out loud to her first. I used her brother as a reason, because it was a poem that was more often taught to a boy.

But when she translated it into her own language, Dutch, she squealed with even more laughter.

It was then that her mother looked at me out of the corner of her eye, and I thought that perhaps I had gone too far.

It went like this in Afrikaans, because I could not speak Dutch, or *Nederlands*, for that matter:

Oupa en Ouma sit op die stoep - *Oupa and Ouma are sitting on the veranda;*

Ouma maak 'n helse poep - *Ouma makes a helluva fart;*

Oupa sê: "wat makeer?" - *Oupa asks, "what is wrong?"*

Ouma sê: "my hol is seer." - *Ouma says, "my arse is sore."*

This was probably one of the naughtiest poems fathers could teach their children when I was young. And it would make many tannies (aunties, or *ontys*) look away in disgust.

Of course, the naughty *tannies* just winked.

And so it sometimes became the reason why it was recited in the first place: to upset some tannies, and to get those naughty tannies on one's side.

I often wondered what was so special about sitting on the stoep and feeling sick.

But of course it was always about the word *poep*. She and her brother understood immediately what *poep* meant, and from then on this took precedence at the dinner table, even over the *ohm* sitting in the *bohm. Boh-ve de strohm.*

Until her mother said it was enough, talking about poep at supper, and so we stopped.

It is interesting, while we are talking about words, now that I am living in North America I have discovered a whole lot of Afrikaans words that people here understand. The Americans talk about their *pinkie* finger. And they often use the word *stoep* as well.

But they pronounce it as one would *stoop* or *group*, which of course is wrong. And this explains why they pronounce *poep* wrongly also. Here in North America dogs make pooops. Not poeps, which is said quickly. As one would say *oop* in oops.

I think we in South Africa shortened the pronunciation in order to save time. It was probably when someone was sitting on the stoep and wanted to make a poep. There was no time to say it the long way, as it stoo-oop, droo-oop or sloo-oop which many people might know is a one-masted sailing yacht.

And it of course makes sense because one would use the word *oops* if one did not get off the stoep quickly enough.

But there are other similar words too.

When I push my golf cart down the fairway some days I feel warm inside when I read the brand name on the handle: *Trekker*.

In fact it will surprise many people, even those who call me Oom, that there are many similarities between American and South African history. The Dutch arrived in their ships not only at Cape Town, but also at New York which they called New Amsterdam. The settlers then both trekked into the interior in ox wagons, with their Bibles in one hand and their guns in the other.

The women even had Voortrekker *kappies*, or bonnets.

They both encountered first-nation people as Canada calls them, and both formed identical laagers with their wagons: these were fortifications in a rectangle or circle for protection.

There were a lot of first-nation people who didn't want them there and so there was a lot of fighting. But instead of using too many bullets, the settlers simply coughed, and their European diseases wiped out most of the local population.

Almost the same thing happened in South Africa: laagers, and fighting. It was not pleasant. Unfortunately for the Boer trekkers, king Shaka was one of the most brilliant military strategists of all time, and things did not go well for them when they trekked into parts of the interior.

But that's a sad part of history, and we didn't talk too much about this at the table when I was young. Instead we stuck very close to innocent images of uncles in trees, and grandmothers farting on the stoep. It was a lot more politically correct, even if it was rude.

As it is, *poep* can mean to fart, as well as the other thing.

I hope you don't have the idea that I am a rude man. Especially when it comes to dating, and because I am now in my sixties.

It is just that, moving here to North America and then losing my wife has not been easy and, to be honest, although I was quite happy to live alone, it was Gord who got me into the dating thing.

And of course Merle, my father's ex-housekeeper from Cape Town.

She said to me one day, "No man should live alone. What about these dating sites? There must be lots of *lekker* - nice - women in America."

Merle always talked about my living in America, even though I told her again and again that Canada is a very different place.

I sometimes talk about North America. And when I use this title, I always think this means America and Canada only.

But living here can be confusing, especially as one gets older, because I have now learnt that even Greenland is included in North America.

And Mexico. But I don't think that they speak the same in Greenland as they do here in Canada. They might even pronounce *Oom* correctly, for instance.

I think that I should go there one day to find out.

But even that would be confusing because when we first came over to settle in Vancouver, we flew over both Greenland and Iceland. Except that Greenland was very icy, and Iceland looked very green, from so high up.

But that was a long time ago, and many things have happened since then.

Who would have said that my Emma would die, and I would be left with such a big hole inside of me?

And then meet so many interesting women? And get into so much trouble, also?

Just when I was planning my trip to Greenland to find out if they say *poep* like we do, I got into dating and then didn't seem to have the time.

2

Women With Small Dogs

I cannot remember if it was Gord or Merle who persuaded me to start dating first.

I think I did say that Merle was my father's housekeeper, from Cape Town.

She has never left Cape Town.

I flew back to South Africa, with Emma's ashes in a jar, and scattered them on the slopes of the oldest mountain in the world - Table Mountain, and she stood next to me there, looking at my wife's ashes blowing in the wind. And I thought of that song, *Blowin' In The Wind*, and the words about how many years before someone can be free. And I thought of how Emma felt free only when we had settled in Canada. For the first time, truly free.

It was there on the slopes of this mountain, just above the city itself, in an old slave house, that she was born and her parents and those before her. Merle still lives there, next door.

Merle always says that South Africa is a world in one country, and just about all the good things in the country are in Cape Town, so there is not ever a reason to go anywhere else.

I think it is just because she is *bang*; she has after all never left her home, and I suspect that underneath all that talk she is more scared than she lets on sometimes. But it is also perhaps because she is a flower seller, and has a number of people working for her: Geraldine, and Stompie. Stoffel, Miriam, Sampie and Daisy.

They all work for her selling flowers at various locations in the city.

She is not always an easy boss to work for, I don't think. I am sure they are a little frightened of her, just as I was of the Little Man, as you will find out later.

When Sampie's son went a little astray and impregnated a girl whose brother was in a gang, Merle took him aside and said, in no uncertain terms, and using words I could not repeat here, but in true South African Cape Flats disciplinary language, that if he went on drugs she would kill him to save the gangs the trouble.

I am sometimes glad I didn't train as a flower seller because when I get something wrong she *skells* me out something terrible. Like when I added chillies to the curry recipe and my date got me into a whole lot of trouble.

More of this later.

But then, in addition to Merle, Gord has also been instrumental in getting me out there with dates.

Long before my wife passed on, I visited the local pool and sauna most days of the week. And that is where I met Gord.

It is a strange place, the sauna. And many strange things happen there.

If you know anything about Canada, you will know it is a very gentle country, and the people are kind, caring and always polite.

And it is as if the pool area is a microcosm of the whole country. In Canada, they are not only gentle and caring people, they are also very cautious.

Even if there are just two people in the pool, there are at least three lifeguards scanning the water for any danger.

One day Gerry collapsed after spending too much time in the sauna.

Everyone was called out of the water. We were told to back off and look the other way. And then they called 911.

So many people arrived, and in so many fire-engines, ambulances and police vehicles, I found it difficult to get out of the parking lot. I was convinced that when I got home I could see a naval destroyer in Semiahmoo Bay. Perhaps it was just the heat of the sauna and the shock of seeing Gerry lying there.

Of course, Merle would have said I was talking *kak*, but in truth I felt that something terrible had happened. And the Canadians have a way of making what we South Africans might consider an element of everyday life look like a spectacle. In truth when a northwester blows gently in Cape Town to clear the air, the Canadians would consider this a storm. So I did not feel that I was overstating things.

At one stage I said I was sure I had heard a helicopter.

Gord did say he had heard nothing.

Anyway Gerry returned four weeks later with three stents in his arteries. Thank goodness, he has not collapsed again.

But now the lifeguards are so afraid something will go wrong that they open the door of the sauna every few minutes to check up on us.

I think they should have a camera, because letting in all that cold air simply made Trevor and George irritated, and I am sure this was the reason for all fracas.

So when Trevor smacked George with his Excel-Power Highthrust fins, knocking his glasses off his head and his book from his lap it was almost not a surprise, as we had witnessed Trevor's irritation each time a lifeguard opened the door to see if everyone was still alive.

But it was surprising in another way, because Trevor is sixty-eight and poor old George is seventy-nine, and one does not normally expect such a thing from two older men.

Apparently George had said something bad to Trevor and he had been waiting for some weeks for the right moment.

It did remind me of a similar incident in Cape Town when I was young.

Oom Athol and Uncle Storky Steyn had ended up getting into a scrap in much the same way. Uncle Storky was a veteran of World War II, and had fought with my father at Tobruk. He was always bragging about his medals, and Oom Athol would then comment that his contribution as a bus driver during the war, in Cape Town, was just as valuable.

Uncle Storky could never get his head around this, and one day called him an *objector*. This made Oom Athol very angry, because he said he had never objected to anything, least of all Storky going up North. It was just all the flashing of his medals he had a problem with.

On this particular day, I shall not easily forget, they had gotten very drunk - in those days during apartheid, men drank alone as no women were allowed inside any bar. Not even if they were white.

That meant that because their women where not there to keep an eye on them, visits to the bar sometimes resulted in drunken incidents, and a few bruises the following day.

Apparently, just before I arrived, Storky Steyn had said that he could get into the lion enclosure, at the zoo up the hill, on the slopes of Table Mountain.

Of course Oom Athol immediately said he was *befok*. This was a very rude word for someone who is crazy.

I happened to be walking home from cricket practice at the time and was standing at the open sash window. They must have seen me because Oom Athol called me.

"Jongman! We need your help."

I was not allowed into the bar, so they came outside to continue their argument, with both of them agreeing that I was to be the referee, on account of the fact that they both respected my father. It was probably because he had won more medals than even Uncle Storky.

By this time Jan Hendricks, also a veteran of the war, but not of Tobruk, joined us. I knew all the war stories, of course, because I was born only ten years after the war ended, in 1955.

Uncle Storky said that he was not talking nonsense and that he would give Oom Athol just about *anything* he wanted if he showed him that he could get into the lion enclosure.

Oom Athol was so confident he was talking *kak*, he even went so far as to say that he would give *Uncle Storky* anything if he did so.

Uncle Storky thought for a moment.

He then said that if he could get into the enclosure, that Oom Athol should follow him inside.

Oom Athol thought about this as he swayed from one side to the other on uncertain feet. And then remembering that there was only one old lion in the enclosure, he agreed.

They shook hands.

But then, for some reason, Oom Storky suddenly seemed hesitant, and said that it could be difficult. This made Oom Athol *very* upset.

He then told Uncle Storky that he was talking even more *kak*, and grabbed my cricket bat, clearly wanting to teach Storky a lesson.

Oom Storky quickly changed his mind, and said that he would definitely do it as agreed. Oom Hendricks quickly grabbed the cricket bat out of Oom Athol's hands and gave it back to me.

But, said Uncle Storky looking Oom Athol straight

in the eye while he stood quite firmly on both legs, if he did actually manage to get inside, Athol should give the lion an enema.

As you can imagine, they were so drunk by this stage that both of them thought this was possible.

Athol looked at him for a long time.

At one point I thought they were going to fall over, but both managed to keep upright. Oom Athol seemed so sure that Storky would never manage even to get inside the lion enclosure that he agreed to this also.

They shook hands again.

But, said Athol, only if Storky held the lion down while he gave him the enema.

Storky said he was quite fine with that. Holding the lion would be no problem, he said.

They went inside and told the barman their plan while I waited for them outside. I could hear the barman chuckle. But he played along anyway, because they came out with a long rubber hose which was normally used to siphon beer from a large barrel to a smaller cask. Two litres of warm beer in a jug, and a large aluminium funnel.

We set off, up the mountain towards the zoo, all four of us. Oom Hendricks carrying the funnel and the hose, Storky carrying the beer. And me carrying my cricket bat.

Although the bar was on the main road of Observatory just below the zoo that was on the slopes of Table Mountain, it was still a long walk.

Halfway up Storky said that he thought it was too far and he refused to carry the jug, so he started to drink the beer.

This set Athol off once again and he started to use many foul swear words in Afrikaans which were much worse than *befok.*

Storky said that he could not believe Athol got upset so quickly, and that it might have been better if instead *he* had been with my father at Tobruk, because he was sure General Rommel might have retreated sooner.

Oom Athol wasn't sure if this was a compliment or not, and grabbed the jug from Storky. This was probably what Storky wanted in the first place.

I held firmly onto my cricket bat just in case.

We set off again, up the hill.

When we finally arrived, the most incredible thing happened.

Uncle Storky, whose name was *Storky* because he walked exactly like a stork, was able to enter through the gate that did not seem to require even a key.

All of us stared at him as he walked inside, and stood on the rock right in the middle of the open lion enclosure.

He put his arms out.

For a moment I thought he looked like General Pienaar, with his arms wide, talking to his troops. General Pienaar was a favourite of my father, so you can imagine how easily this image came to mind.

I could see Athol hesitate.

Storky shouted out, through the wire fence:

"Nee, nee Athol. Jou fok! You must come inside, like you said."

Athol looked very white in the face but walked

through the gate, looking like a stork himself as he gently probed the ground before him.

"*Nou's jou kans, Boet!*" - Now's your chance, Brother!" said Uncle Storky. "Do what you said you would do!"

Out of the corner of my eye, I could see the old lion raise his head and look at the two men - one standing on the rock everyone knew the lion sat on to survey the other animals, and the suburbs of Cape Town below, and the other one approaching as gingerly as a gazelle.

Athol stopped in front of the rock with Storky on it.

We held our breaths.

And then it happened.

Athol said that following Storky inside was enough, and that giving the lion an enema was *onnosel* - stupid.

Now it seemed to me that it was Uncle Storky's turn. Because he, himself, got very upset.

He dropped to the ground, pulled Athol's trousers down and started to give *Oom Athol* the enema.

Athol of course tried frantically to crawl away from the rock, but instead fell to the ground himself. And because he was on his knees, he provided Uncle Storky with the perfect opportunity to carry out the deed.

I do not wish to go into any more details, except to say that by the time the lion had ambled over to see what they were doing, the jug of beer was empty and Oom Athol was lying on his stomach with his arse in the air and a very short rubber hose sticking out.

I cannot tell you what happened after that because I ran down the hill back home with my cricket bat firmly under my one arm and with Oom Hendricks behind me, trying desperately to keep up.

I did not personally witness the fracas between Trevor and George in the sauna that day. I was grateful, as the memory of my visit to the zoo when I was young and the fracas there had been quite enough.

It was Gord who told me the whole story, but suffice it to say that Trevor was then banned from the gym for a month.

I was always grateful to Gord.

Not particularly for the details of the fracas between Trevor and George, but for his tips on dating.

It was he, for instance, who told me never to date women with small dogs.

3

Taking A Peek

"Women with small dogs?" said Gord one day, suddenly. "Keep away from them."

I did not wish him to think that I might be contradicting or challenging him in any way, even by simply asking why it was that they might be dangerous, so I kept very quiet.

Gord sweated some more and then added: "They buy dogs to replace their husbands and, trust me, you'll never have any place in her home. Before you know it, you'll be sleeping on the couch. And you won't be able to go anywhere without the frigging dog."

I looked dead ahead.

"They are all highly bred, shit chocolate and bark at everything."

I contemplated this for some time while I sweated too.

"And the owners are not far off that either," he added.

Gord clearly had had a bad experience.

I decided to visit the water fountain, but before I could get myself off the seat, Gord continued:

"This one time I had a second date with one of them. I think they try to make up for the size of their dogs, I swear..."

I remained tight-lipped.

"She ordered three glasses of French wine at $20 per glass, on *my* credit card, and then when we got back to her place, she took out some crap that didn't cost more than $8 a bottle."

I cleared my throat, as if to show some sympathy.

"Then we took *Foo-Foo* for a walk. I have never seen such a dump - I swear it was bigger than the dog! And then she expected *me* to carry the poop in the bag. When I said I didn't know her, or her dog that well, she asked me if it was because I didn't like animals!"

Gord had never shared as much before. I could see that his experience had not been a good one.

A lifeguard peered inside through the window. It is likely that they felt partly responsible for the fracas between Trevor who was now banned from the gym for a month, and George who was sitting next to me on the right reading his book, and so no longer opened the door each time.

We were grateful.

"Make sure you check on their profile. There will always be a picture of a small dog somewhere. Usually up against their face. And they're all so frigging ugly too," he added.

I assumed Gord meant the dog and not necessarily the women.

By this time Gord had managed to get me onto *Match.com, Plenty Of Fish* and a few other sites. My favourite was *POF*, although now looking back, and because I no longer have any need for these sites, I cannot tell you why.

I think it was probably because it was free.

Not that I want you to think that I am cheap, even though my friend, Johan, a doctor originally from Oudtshoorn in the Klein Karoo said that he felt I might appear as such, at times.

I did feel a little insulted, but I also felt that maybe he had a point. I had told him the story about one of my first interactions. A very nice looking women by the name of Celia from North Vancouver who had answered a *wink* I had sent her (you can send people winks without any words, or commitment). She seemed quite keen on phoning me which I had thought was very nice.

I was to find out, later, that this was unusual.

I sent her my number and she phoned me one Saturday morning. We chatted for a while and then she suggested we meet somewhere for lunch.

For some reason I became a little suspicious.

The first meeting is always something like sharing coffee, or perhaps just a walk somewhere. But it is not seen as the first *date*.

Gord had been very specific.

I decided to follow his lead and asked her whether she considered the first meeting a date or simply a meeting.

She seemed hesitant, but then did answer: "I think it is a bit of both."

After a respectful pause, I then asked if it was just a meeting also, whether she felt we should share the bill.

I was careful to say this gently, like the Canadians do, and not in a pushy South African way.

The phone call ended abruptly.

I was left with two trains of thought for some time afterwards. One from Gord who said: "I told you so - she's just a serial dater, and goes from one lunch date to another. You would have paid for the lunch, and never heard from her again."

There was also the opinion of Johan when next I sat on his stoep at the back of his house and had a beer with him.

"You never talk about money on the first date," he said. Then he looked at me, and quickly added, "or the first meeting."

I sat without saying anything because I felt that Johan should know about these things. He had only been divorced once, and his father had also been a doctor. And also coming from Oudtshoorn which had been a very rich town when Ostrich feathers were popular, and not Observatory in Cape Town, he probably knew better.

When Merle skyped me that night she said that she wasn't sure who should pay for what, but that a flowers were always a good thing.

And so with this in mind, I always stopped somewhere to buy a flower or two.

It was to Zoe that I took the first flower, a small tulip, one day.

She was, during all the time of dating, the only woman who ever contacted me first. She mentioned that she was impressed with my reference to *intellectual stimulation*.

It had been Johan, and not Gord who had alerted me to this. It might be tempting to talk about physical attraction, but he had said that this was not what most women were looking for. Only.

I thought that coming from Oudtshoorn he knew best so had included the fact, in my profile, that I felt the other kind of stimulation was just as important.

Besides, I had noticed an *Emily-lu* from Port Moody whose subtitle read, *"Sincere men seem to be odsolete. How much truth is this?"*

It spurred me on to believe that maybe Johan was right, and I decided it was important that I should come across as *sincere*. And talking about physical stuff up front is perhaps not the way to go about this.

Zoe had emailed me to say that she liked my profile and thought we should meet.

When I read this I was encouraged because I thought that I was getting the hang of things.

Even Gord said that it is quite rare for women to email first, that they rather wait for the man to email them, or give them a wink before responding.

I scanned all three of her pics for dogs and found none. After three or four emails we set about finding a place to meet.

I could tell from the way she said things that she also saw this first meeting as just a meeting.

We agreed on False Creek which is probably my favourite place next to the Waterfront in Cape Town. One can spend hours walking around, looking out across the water at the boats and the apartments on the other side. And when one gets tired, a ride on a water taxi is even more exciting.

So we met for coffee at a local pub, right on the water.

I paid.

After we had walked all the way to Science World and back, she said she would like to see me again. It would be my first real date, apart from some meetings and two lunches.

So we made a date for that Saturday evening. I was sure the flower had done it.

I took her more flowers - this time two tulips.

I think she was delighted.

I found parking which can be difficult in Vancouver and can also result in one's car easily being towed away, and a fine costing more than three dates.

We had agreed on Mahony & Sons again.

We sat on the deck downstairs, and looked out over the water with the sun catching the windows of the apartments on the other side and turning them into mirrors that looked as though they were made of gold.

There was a thin blanket of snow on the mountains above them, and we chatted about the beautiful vistas Vancouver offered so abundantly while we enjoyed a delicious dinner and some wine.

Then we walked some way around False Creek once again, and caught a water taxi back to the opposite side of the creek.

I felt my heart beating when she slipped her hand into mine; just like a teenager, I was worried that my hand might be sweaty. Even though it was cool outside and I began to feel I was in the sauna back at the pool.

This worried me because I could recall a long conversation Merle and I had had, on skype, about hot flushes.

I made a mental note to ask Johan if men could also get them.

Before I knew it, we were standing outside an apartment building, just one street up from False Creek. I had hardly noticed, holding so tightly onto Zoe's hand like that.

"Would you like to come up for some coffee?" asked Zoe.

Gord had said that I would know that things were going right if they invited me in for coffee.

Or something else.

I was almost breathless from expectation and, all I could do was nod. She led me inside, through the fancy front doors, and up in an elevator that seemed to have been decorated by family of a Spanish conquistador.

It was when she opened her front door that I felt things had turned around for the worst.

There on the floor, staring up at us, was the smallest, scruffiest looking dog I had ever seen.

In the olden days before they genetically engineered fruit, mangoes were very stringy. And when one had finished eating a mango, one was left with a pip and an untidy bunch of stringy hairs that jutted outwards into the air at all angles, and that always reminded me of the flames from rockets.

This dog looked just like a mango pip.

As I stared at him I was hoping that the *flames* were not the result of a desperate attempt by fleas to escape from his body.

In addition to his untidy appearance, he had one black eye and one blue one.

In fact after sitting down to recover, and eyeing him myself for a while I became convinced that Zoe could make money by casting him in an alien movie.

Of course I didn't say anything to her about alien movies. I was mindful of the fact that I was there to give her intellectual stimulation, as I had claimed in my profile, and not advice about her dog.

While she poured us a drink I sat looking at him.

He sat at my feet, staring up at me.

After a while I noticed that his left eye was not only blue, but that it was also squint. One small tooth also stuck out, and a portion of his tongue dangled to one side, out of the corner of his mouth.

I think he assumed I was startled in noticing all this, and felt sorry for me, because he tried to pacify me with a tiny, friendly growl. Even when he did, his tongue did not go back into his mouth.

"He's my Little Man," said Zoe. "I couldn't do without him. He keeps me company, listens to my stories and welcomes me home each day after work."

I asked what he did all day while she was at work.

"Oh, he goes to doggie day care," she said. "It's a little expensive - $500 a month - but the Little Man deserves the best, don't you think?" she said, as she put a glass of whisky in my hand.

I took a small sip and immediately felt better.

At eight thousand Rands a month, I imagined Merle could keep at least two families alive in Cape Town.

Zoe sat down next to me. I wondered what would happen next.

I soon found out.

It is amazing how women seem to treat couches. No man may ever puts his shoes or feet on a couch, as Merle and my deceased wife always told me, but here in Canada, or perhaps with a newer generation, women today lift their feet and curl them under their buttocks or a blanket on any couch.

It looked very inviting when she did that, and I took another sip of whisky.

For a while we spoke about the difference between whisky and whiskey. Thankfully I knew that one was Scottish and the other Irish, even though I could not remember which one.

I told her that the best way to drink whisky was to drink it neat without ice, because the ice bruises the whisky. And to pour into the glass a teaspoon of water to release the flavours. I then commented on the peatiness of the taste and suggested that it might come from the Isle of Islay.

She squealed with delight and said I had guessed the exact place. I did not want to tell her that it was pure luck that I had recognised the taste.

I think Zoe was impressed because she moved closer to me and before long I discovered that my right arm was on the couch behind her and my hand was hanging over her shoulder.

When I realised, after a third sip, that my fingers were neatly fitted over her small breast, I quickly sat more upright and took my hand away. It's amazing what a few tots of whisky can do, I thought.

But Zoe must have seen the position of my hand as a good sign, because she unfolded her legs from under her, got up and beckoned me to follow her.

When I did lean forward to get up off the couch, I felt a tiny pressure on my foot. When I looked down I realised that the *Little Alien* had his behind resting on my shoe. I was grateful that when we came into the apartment, Zoe had said not to worry about taking my shoes off, which is what Canadians usually do before they enter their home.

Zoe disappeared down the passage.

I leant forward and very gently, so as not to upset the Little Man, nudged him off.

I followed Zoe down to the end of the corridor. There I found her bedroom.

By this time the whisky was beginning to have some effect and I even found myself commenting favourably on the many pictures of her and the Little Man on the walls all around me.

Before I knew what was happening I was lying down on the bed next to Zoe. I had a warm feeling, lying there. We were alone and it was comforting to smell the aromas of lavender and peach in the room.

I exhaled deeply, closed my eyes and began to float as though I were one of the yachts tied to a buoy in False Creek, with just a gentle current that lifted and dropped me every now and then.

Suddenly I heard a soft thud.

I raised my head and found I was looking straight into the blue, squint eye of the *Little Alien*. He had taken position in the middle of a bench covered in furry fabric, at the foot of the bed. He was staring at me with his head cocked to the left. I became convinced that with the weight of the squint, and also the dangling tongue pulling him in one direction, that this was why his head was bent over to the left.

I took a slow, deep breath and lowered my head onto the pillow again.

Zoe seemed very comfortable. In fact, so comfortable she leaned over and began to tickle my ear with her tongue. I was immediately reminded of the kiss she had given the dog when we entered the apartment, and hoped that the whisky had had some effect not only on her mood, but also on her mouth.

It was a strange sensation, the tickling, and soon I realised that the entire tip of her tongue was inside my ear.

"I don't mind some nookie," she said, taking her tongue out of my ear, "but I must just tell you that when we're finished, and you do perhaps get to sleep over, it will have to be in the spare room."

I was determined not to show my ignorance in asking what *nookie* meant, because I felt I was getting a handle on the whole dating scene, and imagined I knew what it was.

At least, if I was to sleep over, I could do so alone without the Little Man between us. Or staring at me from the foot of the bed.

Zoe whispered into my ear, after licking it once again, "Just pretend to fall asleep and he'll go away."

I lay as still as I could with my eyes closed.

I don't know if it was the whisky, or the fact that I had brought her two flowers, or just that it was having a man lie down beside her, but she soon fell fast asleep.

All that talk of nookie, me sleeping over, and whisky must have been just too much for her.

I lay there contemplating my future with Zoe. And the Little Man.

When Zoe started snoring I decided that perhaps The Universe was giving me a sign.

I slipped off the bed as easily as the Little Man had slid off my shoe, and made my way down the short passage to the front door. Behind me I could hear the soft thud of a tiny body landing on the floor of the bedroom, and then the pitter-patter of little feet on the tiles all the way to the kitchen and the front door.

What happened there reinforced my idea that Gord knew exactly what he was talking about when it came to small dogs because when I looked down, just before I closed the door, there was the *Little Alien* sitting on his butt, staring up at me.

I cannot tell you for certain whether it was just the image of the mango pip that did it.

Or if it was the three tots of that deliciously peaty whisky I had in my stomach, but when I looked down at him he seemed to have swapped eyes.

The right eye was now blue, and squint. And the left one was now black. In addition to this his tongue was now dangling down the right side of his face, rather than the left, having followed the squint.

I know, after talking to Johan, my doctor friend, a few days later, that this is impossible but I have decided to record these incidents just as I remember them.

In addition to the fact that they had swapped places, the right eye, which was now blue, went especially squint.

But it was not just that it went squint.

It was that it went *so* squint, and his tongue dangled out so far, that the poor little fellow fell right over onto his side.

I felt so sorry for him, that when I did relate part of the encounter to Gord the following day in the sauna, I referred to the dog as neither *Little Alien* nor the *Mango Pip*, but respectfully as the Little Man.

Gord just said, "I told you so."

And that was the end of it.

We never said anything about small dogs again.

4

Three Kings From Afar

I told Gord a few days later that I felt it was truly remarkable how much going on dates reminded me of things back in South Africa.

He simply nodded.

Take Jennifer and Sinterklaas, for example.

And how that reminded me of the three kings on donkeys that special night all those years before.

Now that was something I remembered well, I said to myself while I sat next to Gord, grateful that there would be no more talk of small dogs.

Jennifer was, is a kindergarten teacher.

Amazingly, we did not meet online at all.

In fact we had been introduced by one of Emma's friends right here in White Rock, British Columbia.

At first I was apprehensive because when I did talk to any of Emma's friends I was, as you can imagine, always reminded of her.

And how she had died.

I was no longer frightened of blind dates simply because, what with all those meeting-dates, I felt comfortable walking into a venue and looking around for the person I was supposed to meet, having not met them before.

In fact I was so used to this, that I realised that the second date was never quite as exciting as the first. Funny how our brains work sometimes.

Jennifer was far from dull.

In fact she burst into a big smile when I walked onto the deck of Hemmingways in White Rock, overlooking the bay, and across at the little town of Blaine in Washington, USA.

I know that you might think that I had chosen Hemmingways because of the remarkable Innis & Gunn - a beer matured in whiskey oak casks, and in my opinion one of the best beers in the world. And a beer that I felt some higher power itself had offered to me in place of those bitter pale ale and IPA's. Of course I did not suggest this to Merle who, I am sure, would have given me a lengthy description of how God's powers work.

But I had not suggested this place, because I had said to Emma's friend that Jennifer should choose whatever venue she felt comfortable with. As you can see I was wanting to handle this carefully so as to make a good impression with Emma's friend as I knew everything would get back to her.

But I must tell you, I was grateful when we messaged one another, and she suggested we meet there.

She said she would be wearing a red and white

blouse and would have a hat. At first I was apprehensive, because I remembered the red and white Bel Air that fateful day when I met Sharon and Sparky.

Jennifer was sitting quietly, up against the railing and looking out across the bay. She did indeed have a red and white top on and it shimmered in the afternoon sun. A white scarf drifted down her back from her cream coloured hat. She painted quite a picture, but I secretly hoped that the red and white colours did not signal the start of anything too dramatic.

But then I relaxed because I remembered that she was a kindergarten teacher.

I bent down, and kissed her on her cheek. Very lightly, so as not to cause any alarm.

She smiled. "This is such a nice spot, don't you think?" She had her head cocked to one side as she looked up at me.

I said I did.

"Have you tried their Innis & Gunn?"

I laughed.

When I told her that it was my favourite beer she giggled, and touched my arm. I felt warm inside and got the idea that we could be good together.

I sat with my back to the setting sun and looked out at the boats in the bay while Jennifer told me about herself.

Jennifer bounced this way and that in her chatty manner and after some time she apologised, touched my arm again, and asked me something about myself.

I smiled and told her that I had studied to be a teacher many years before. And that I felt strongly, and quite sincerely, that pre-school teachers were the real heroes of our society and should be paid more than teachers of other grades.

After all, I said, our personalities are fully formed by around six years of age, as was our intelligence too. And I felt this meant that pre-school was the most critical period.

"Oh, I know!" she said, laughing out aloud. "That's amazing. Anyone would think you were my principal! It's a pity other people don't fully realise this."

I know what you are thinking, but I did genuinely feel this to be true.

Jennifer looked at me. "Would you...; would you like to help me with something? I know this is the first date. I mean, meeting. Oh, I feel a bit stupid! But I. I was...."

I touched her hand, lightly. I told her it was okay, she could just come out with it and it would be fine.

"Well, I'm looking for a Sinterklaas! Do you know what that is?"

I told her that I did because I had spent some time, as a student, in the Netherlands and had attended a little pageant at a primary school many years before.

She raised her hands to her cheeks and clapped them with delight.

"Oh! That's amazing! Just truly amazing..."

And then she became almost quiet. "You know," she said. "I had such a good feeling about coming here to meet you?"

I might have been wrong, but looking back now, I am sure she winked at me.

"So you can help me, then? We choose two cultural events each year, so that the kids can get exposure to cultures from around the world. And this time we're doing Sinterklaas."

She looked at me, as though it was my turn.

I took a small sip of my Innis & Gunn, mindful of the fact that it's alcohol contents was 7%, and I smiled at her.

"I need..., I mean, could you possibly agree to being Sinterklaas? What with your experience and all that. I know the kids are going to love it."

I said I would.

I had no idea that it involved almost the entire outfit which can sometimes be tricky. What with the long red cape. And the long white beard. A red mitre and a ruby ring. Not to mention the shepherd's staff.

When they dressed me in the gymnasium I felt so weighed down I wondered whether I might make it down the passage to the main hall where the kids were waiting - there with a tree of presents and tables laden with food.

In addition to the heavy ring and the shepherd's mitre, I was asked to carry a large book. It had the names of the kids, and my job was to look them up and read a list of achievements.

I was not given any helper. Least of all a black one, which would normally have been a Zwarte Piet who would have carried both a bag of sweets for the good kids, and a chimney sweep's broom made of willow branches, and used to spank naughty children.

There was, of course, no spanking of kids in Canada. And we don't have too many willows, either.

After having done some research, I found out that some of the Sinterklaas songs talk about putting kids in a bag and sending them to Spain. But no one really knows what Spain has got to do with it.

Frankly, when it gets cold in Canada, I imagine that any child would endure anything in order to get to Spain.

But I was told not to mention this because a child had been abducted, in Ontario in 1996, and talk of moving children around in bags was not a preferred subject to speak about in front of them.

Especially in Canada.

The ceremony went off very well.

Except that one child asked why I had not arrived on a white horse.

I felt put out.

I mumbled something through my beard, but the teacher quickly offered the explanation that no horses were allowed on school premises. Besides, she said, they didn't have big enough poop-bags for horses.

The boy seemed content with this explanation.

In place of Zwarte Piet, two teachers came to my aid, and I paged through the book and whispered something to them before they handed out the presents.

I sat there sweating in my heavy outfit, wondering what the teachers intended doing with the naughty kids.

I decided though, after reading the achievements of some of them, that there were probably none.

For some reason, I could not get a picture of me on a white horse out of my mind for the rest of that day.

And it made me think of my mother's nativity play in Greyton, back home in South Africa.

When we had lived on Robben Island, she had insisted on organising one in the small stadium. It involved almost everyone living on the island at the time except the prisoners, of course, who in those days were not political prisoners, and walked the island in work details, often visiting me.

I had been the boy that had held the donkey still, while Mary was lifted onto its back. And I could remember the experience as though it were yesterday.

The tiffies - electrical technicians in the Navy (it was a naval base at the time) - had even managed to illuminate the archangel's wings and with the lights off in the stadium that night the angel had lit up to such a degree that my Nanny, a Xhosa woman from the Transkei, screamed with delight, telling us afterwards that she was sure the angel was Catholic.

How so? my mother had asked afterwards.

Because just like the bread that became the body of Christ, so this electrified angel walking into the stadium in darkness and then having his wings flood the grounds had, at least for a moment, become the real archangel Michael.

From then on we were all suitably impressed with Mary's observations. And it occurred to me that perhaps in a previous life Nanny and Merle had met, because as you will find out Merle is an expert on angels.

Years later, when Nanny left us, Merle had come into our lives as our housekeeper.

And so it was that, one day, my mother told Merle all about the nativity play on the island.

And Merle must have thought about it for a long time and when my parents retired to the small town, far from Robben Island, called Greyton she and my mother decided to stage another one.

Because my father had become mayor, my mother was determined to involve him in some way. But because he was not religious, and in fact especially disliked dominees - pastors - whom he claimed adopted mournful, dour looks on their faces when pronouncing the wages of sin, he was adamant that he not be Joseph, or any kind of angel.

"Wat van een van die 3 kings?" What about one of the three kings? said Merle one day as they sat down with the large sewing box, and a number of robes and nativity paraphernalia.

My mother raised her eyebrows.

That meant they needed three donkeys or horses, and two more men. They looked at me, but I was to be Joseph, so I shook my head.

My mother approached my father that evening at dinner. He seemed to finish his meal with some apathy.

But he did agree as it was for my mother. I think he felt partly relieved that it was not in any way a religious role. I think his dislike of anything religious had stemmed from an early childhood memory he had once shared with me.

Apparently coming back from a church service during which the dominee had suggested that because of sin in the community the drought had been particularly bad, it had rained.

They had spent half the time groaning over the consequences of their sin, and the other half of the service praying for the rain so badly needed.

On the way back to the farm, unfortunately it had rained so heavily the crops were destroyed. My father, apparently, had piped up from the back of the ox-wagon, that they had probably prayed too hard.

His mother had insisted he be tied to a pole and whipped.

I felt that it was a good idea he sat on a donkey or a horse, with some exotic and colourful attire my mother and Merle would conjure up, rather than be on the ground anywhere near baby Jesus or angels, just in case he might recall that whipping.

But then again, my father was not a vengeful man at all.

There remained the problem of finding two other kings.

Emma was of course Mary, and to complement her beautiful Mediterranean toned complexion, and to be both politically and socially correct, Merle had actually found a live baby in the town next door that looked very black.

The stage was set.

But we were still missing two kings.

My father disappeared while all further arrangements were made, and the frantic activities took place - costumes, candles, music.

The wooden manger he constructed in the workshop took longer than it might have done. I am sure this was the case because he did not want to be too involved in the rest of the fuss. Especially if it involved anything religious. Not that he said anything; it was just that I knew him well.

I think that when the other two kings were finally

found, he might have been sorry for not making himself more available, and perhaps in another role.

In true Merle-style she had managed to think of something that would challenge, and heal at the same time.

She was good at this, and I think deep down, just as Zwarte Piet was Sinterklaas's helper, she definitely felt that she was more than a housekeeper and assistant to my parents alone - I was always convinced she felt she had the same position with God Himself.

"Weet jy wat twee maande gelede by ons kerk gebeur het?" she asked my mother. Do you know what happened two months ago at our church?

My mother stopped sewing, and looked up. She knew, instinctively, there was something important about to be revealed.

There always was with Merle.

"Ons dominee het die wit dominee gevra vir stoele vir 'n groot gathering by ons." Our pastor asked the white pastor for some chairs for a big gathering at our church.

"Can you believe it? He said no. *Hulle wou nie kleurlinge op hulle stoele hé nie...!"* They didn't want coloured people sitting on their chairs!

My mother shook her head.

I looked at my father who had just walked in. And right there, I knew that Merle was up to something.

And somehow I knew that my father would regret first moving to Greyton, second becoming mayor. And third agreeing to help Merle and my mother. Not that there had ever been a chance of avoiding that.

One did not say no to my mother. And certainly not

to Merle. She ruled our house with an iron rod bigger than that of Sinterklaas.

She waited for my father to leave the room, bent over and whispered to my mother:

"Jy moet die wit dominee vra om die een king te wees. Ek vra vir ons dominee..." You ask the white dominee to be the one king, and I'll ask our pastor...

My mother stopped sewing, again.

And then they both burst out laughing.

"Ja," said Merle. *"Vir sy sondes, kan die dominee saam met ons s'n ry. Miskien sal hy leer om saam met ander mense op stoele to sit!"* For his sins, the dominee can ride with our pastor. Perhaps he will learn to sit with others on chairs!

Neither Merle nor my mother wasted any time. I could hear my mother's honey voice smooth-talking the white dominee on the phone. The next day Merle came back from the village smiling.

"Ons dominee sê ja!" He says yes! "And he didn't ask who the other kings were. I told him we had only one donkey so far.

It was a white lie and I wondered what Merle would have to say for it, when she stood before God one day.

Greyton had many horses and donkeys. In fact they often wandered around looking for company.

The evening of the grand nativity play arrived; most of the villagers showed up with food and clothing donations for the poor, and also wrapped gifts for the local schools in the area, especially the one in Genadendal, the next town that was not quite as affluent as Greyton.

It was a huge success.

Not least of all when my father the mayor, beautifully attired, rode into the garden on a donkey, only just behind a surprised looking dominee and Merle's smiling pastor with a big smile on his face, and who seemed to be the only one who was fully enjoying the irony.

Merle had not gotten her entire way; my father had refused to wear his mayoral chain, even though it looked as though it was made of gold.

If nothing else, their arrival elicited a round of applause which in fact startled the archangel who was behind the small covering under which our black Jesus lay.

This in turn made the baby Jesus cry.

Luckily, Emma, who was then still my girlfriend, came to the rescue and picked him up in her arms.

I think that somehow God and Merle had worked perfectly together that day, because not only did the three kings end well, but it was the sight of Emma holding that beautiful baby that made me realise I wanted to spend the rest of my life with her.

We all settled down again with the baby Jesus falling asleep, right there in my father's manger.

And although dismounting was somewhat difficult for the three men in their robes, my mother and Merle both insisted the three kings approach the crib and place their gifts at the baby's feet.

It is ironic but that is the only time I could ever remember my father looking as dismal as the dominee himself, that night as he rode into our garden on his donkey.

But he redeemed himself, and when mounted again and on his way out, he leant over and said something to the other two kings.

I never found out what it was, but they exited, all laughing.

And Merle was happy to report that there was no longer any problem borrowing chairs from the white church.

In fact, before my mother and Merle could eke out any more revenge the following year, Merle reported that the coloured congregation she belonged to, and the white Dutch Reformed church had started having combined services once a month.

Indeed, God moves in mysterious ways, I thought to myself, when I remembered the donkey I had held steady for Mary that day as a child on Robben Island, and I decided that clearly God favoured donkeys above all else and that when they were involved, mighty things always happened.

And so you can see the reason the image of riding a horse became so clear to me - not least of all when, now, many years later, I was almost duped into riding one myself.

And, no, I do not mean at the school.

My appearance as Sinterklaas was apparently so successful that Jennifer's children asked if they could do it again.

I am not sure whether Jennifer assumed that we, as a couple, would still be together, or perhaps she felt time between us was running out, but without giving too many details I can only say the following: we spent many interesting hours with me in my Sinterklaas outfit, alone, on her small holding in Langely.

Exactly how we managed to get the outfit off and what we did after it lay on the floor I feel, because I could never give such details to Merle or my mother, it would not be appropriate for me to share them here either.

It was fun, as you might imagine.

Especially when I kept the large white beard on.

But sadly, I think Jennifer became too obsessed with the idea of me in my Sinterklaas outfit.

And of me taking it off.

One Friday evening during one of our sessions, I felt that it was time to say goodbye.

Jennifer had decided that she would catch one of the neighbour's donkeys, and have me ride it into her courtyard suitably mounted and in my Sinterklaas outfit, while she was tied to the olive tree.

I felt that she was taking this too far, and that it was, perhaps, time to end the fun and games.

I somehow did not wish to indulge Jennifer's desire, even though I had been determined to make a good impression.

I could somehow not see myself, in her courtyard, on the back of a donkey. Not even, I felt, if God Himself had a particularly profound revelation to share with me when I did.

I think that little voice within me, saying it was time to exit, was enough to be the motivator. Whether it was indeed God's, or just mine.

And so it was that Jennifer and I went our separate ways.

She, of course, managed to find someone else.

I knew this because there, in the Peace Arch News the next year, was Jennifer smiling up at a large handsome Sinterklaas.

I felt he did not paint a picture as handsome as me, but to be fair he sat the donkey very well, up against the blue Canadian sky, as he rode through the gates of Jennifer's small school.

I assumed they had found a poop-bag big enough, or the city bylaws had changed.

And, strangely, it was a donkey that seemed to look as if it might be very comfortable anywhere it went.

I am a little embarrassed to even admit this but I wondered, looking at the picture in the newspaper, whether that donkey itself had perhaps seen the inside of a courtyard on a few occasions.

And it occurred to me, thinking of Jennifer, and of my mother and of Merle. And of those three kings that day. That it is often amazing what men will do to please a woman.

5

A Fit

Gord had given me a clear warning about small dogs.

But he had never mentioned anything about cars, or larger dogs.

There can be no doubt, coming to North America, that men - and sometimes women - love their cars.

One of my favourite pastimes is to sit on the deck of a pub in White Rock, on a warm evening, and watch the parade of vehicles up and down the strip.

All manner of cars come to the fore. Hotrods, exotic speedsters, and the moneyed showing off with their Lamborghinis, Ferraris and Maseratis.

In Cape Town before sanctions, my father had had many cars including a Studebaker that was the talk of our neighbourhood. I became famous when I took special friends out for a ride, and asked my father to stop on an incline. The marvel of the particular model

Studebaker was that it had an automatic brake, so that the car remained stationary without the driver having to put his foot on the brake pedal.

On most Saturday afternoons my father would take a short drive to get wood, beer and meat for a braai - barbeque - later in the day. There would usually be a long line-up of little boys hoping to go for a ride in the car.

And in the line-up one could hear, when my father started the engine, *Jislaaik, man! Jislaaik!* - Jeez-man!

They would gladly pay me for the privilege of sitting in front, in the passenger seat, so that when my father stopped on an incline and the car did not slide backwards, they could bend down, and later vouch for the fact that he did not move his foot from the accelerator.

It became a topic of discussion so far and wide that many years later when I was almost twenty, and in between going to the Angolan border to fight the Cubans, I was sitting having a vodka, lime and lemonade with my girlfriend Emma in a pub in Greenpoint when I heard someone at the table next to us discussing this phenomenon.

I remember how impressed she was when I told her they were talking about my father.

Even though this was Greenpoint, and Greenpoint was a suburb of Cape Town, and Cape Town was the most progressive city that often defied the apartheid laws, I had to keep her chatting to take her mind off the fact that as a non-white, she should not be there.

Strictly speaking we were not allowed to date one another, because I was classified as white.

I remember looking at Emma sitting on the stool in the soft evening light at the restaurant, and thinking that when one starts with something unnatural it results in many complications and difficulties.

And so I chatted about all the cars my father had owned, and those he had restored, like the 1935 8hp two-seater Morris Tourer that he had found on Oom Kiepie Cronje's (pronounced *Kron-year's*) chicken farm in Phillipi.

It was just a *kipiehok* - a chicken coop - and Pa and I had spent many evenings restoring it.

Or the 1948 Rover I had learnt to drive in.

What about two-tone 1958 Oldsmobile that could accommodate ten of us boys in the boot? I asked.

I kept her busy listening to me while we drank our vodkas, and before we left to go see *Deliverance* at the local bioscope.

That was also a challenge because the non-whites usually sat upstairs and the whites downstairs, which always seemed to me ironic discrimination.

Depending on the usher, we had to make a decision as to whether I could pass for coloured or she would pass for white. The decision would then result in us going upstairs or remaining down.

Those were heady day for us, the early seventies. What with critical decisions such as these to make every time we went out.

But it didn't matter to Emma and me because we were in love.

Only once did we have our tickets taken away because we refused to be separated, when an old usher recognised us as being, one coloured, and the other white.

Even though we were used to a system that separated people, Emma was in tears when we walked home that evening.

I put my arm around her and said that we would think of something, even though I had no idea what to do.

Luckily I had just got my licence and, at home, when I told Pa what had happened he gave me the keys to the Oldsmobile.

My heart beat wildly.

So much so I was worried, when I got into the driver's seat, that it would come flying out of my chest.

But it all worked out for the best because I drove Emma up to the top of Signal Hill.

There we sat on the wide bench of the front seat, and looked down at the shimmering lights of Greenpoint and Seapoint below us. And out, in the darkness, to the flickering lights of Robben Island.

It was there, on that hill, that Emma and I truly kissed for the first time. I was so giddy with excitement - what with my heart beating so much, sitting in that great Oldsmobile, and the kiss itself - that the next day I went to the bioscope and kissed the mean old usher on the cheek to thank him for being so mean.

But when I told Emma this she was not impressed with me. And I had to wait a few weeks before she kissed me properly again.

With such wonderful memories of dating in Cape Town when I was young I often sit, today, with an Innis & Gunn beer, in a special designer beer glass in deference to the parade of vehicles down the strip on Marine Drive, in White Rock, British Columbia. And I think of my Emma.

On one such evening I noticed a teenager driving a McLaren 675LT.

Although I am not one for sitting in public and playing with an electronic device, I did quickly consult Google and learned that this car has a horsepower rating of exactly 666.

I took a very small sip of the beer, on account of the fact that even though I was able to walk the short distance back home, the beer did have an alcohol content of over 7%.

In fact it was like the beer equivalent of a McLaren 675LT.

Taking that sip, I felt as though I might be sitting in the car itself, with the smell of leather all around me.

The McLaren grumbled its way past me.

It was so low that I imagined the driver's buttocks could not be more than six inches above the road. I tried to imagine what six hundred and sixty-six horsepower could do to a young man's butt. Or the butt of a man of my age.

And once again I thought about the enema that Uncle Storky had given Oom Athol, and whether his butt ever did fully recover.

And the 666 reminded me of the time Merle got mixed up with some evangelical group. We used to call them chandelier swingers on account of the fact that when the *spirit* got hold of them, after much chanting and shouting, they went a little wild.

And when the *spirit* had arrived, there was always talk of The Beast. And I remember how it was that this Beast would rule the world one day with his signature number: 666.

I could only imagine what it must be like with the *spirit* inside one, although I was always too frightened to try.

Merle said it was like having a *you-know-what*, but in a religious sort of way.

I have often wondered what she meant.

But sitting there on that veranda, with the golden sun bouncing off the water in the bay, and half a glass of Innis & Gunn inside me, and that McLaren rumbling by, I could imagine that putting one's foot down on the accelerator, on an open road, must indeed be something like the *spirit* taking hold of one.

And so it was one day that Sharon from Abbotsford popped up on my Plenty Of Fish screen saying in her profile that she was interested only in men who knew about cars.

I thought of my drive with Emma up to Signal Hill and the restoration of the Morris and all the other cars, and felt I might perhaps fit such requirements, so I replied.

She met me for coffee in Abbotsford.

I immediately thought that she was very good looking, although a bit short. Her hair was red and her eyes were green, and she wore a very colourful blouse that was red and white. She certainly stood out in a crowd and I got to thinking that this seemed to make up for her lack of height.

I told her she looked nice.

And then we arranged for the first date at Cosmos, a Greek restaurant in White Rock.

I walked there because, as I said, I lived down the road. But Sharon arrived in a red and white 1955 Chevrolet Bel Air Convertible.

Jislaaik! What a car *that* was.

I started telling her about Pa's cars, and slowly built up to the climax - when I told her I was born in 1955 she got so excited I thought she might have an *accident* sitting right there in the restaurant.

It was perhaps then that I should have heard at least a few warning bells.

But I was so taken with the car, and even more with her appreciation of the fact that I had stories about so many others, I got the idea that we were very compatible.

Sharon arranged for a drive down the strip the following Friday evening in the Bel Air. It would be the perfect time because my weather app said it was going to be sunny.

I had promised that after the ride I would take her to dinner at any restaurant she might choose. She gave me a kiss on the cheek and smiled broadly, and I was convinced we were becoming more and more compatible. I could feel my heart beat just a little faster.

I thought of the car every day that week, and alerted some of my friends, Johan and even Gord that I would be parading down the strip in it, at around 6:30.

"Do you think she will let you drive the car?" asked Gord.

I said that I didn't mind if she did not because it would be a treat just to sit next to her and wave at them.

I could hardly wait for Friday to arrive.

In preparation for the event I decided to make sure I was dressed properly.

Because the Bel Air was half red and Sharon seemed to like red blouses, I took out, from the back of my closet, my red velskoen (shoes from skin).

I cleaned them thoroughly and made sure the laces were not frayed and that they tied neatly. In addition, I had bought a new pair of dark blue jeans that I felt would set the red velskoene off.

And a white shirt.

And because I was also Canadian, I put on a Canucks baseball cap.

I was ready for Sharon and her Bel Air.

Unfortunately, after all that waiting, when she finally arrived on time, I was a little deflated.

I had pictured the two of us driving up and down the strip in that beautiful car together, with me sitting beside her.

If Gord had warned me about little dogs, he had said nothing about large ones.

When she pulled up outside in the driveway I noticed there was someone sitting next to her in the front.

When I looked a little more closely I realised it was one of the largest dogs I had seen. It was even larger than Sergeant-Major De Beer's giant Poodle who was the parade mascot at the Wynberg Military Base in Cape Town when I was a child.

In South Africa, probably because of apartheid and sanctions, we were perhaps not so informed about international terminology and trends.

I always thought that the small Poodles were the normal size, and the large ones were called *giant*. We had no idea that large Poodles were the normal size, and the smaller ones were miniature.

Sergeant-Major De Beer's Poodle was definitely the *giant* version.

He led each parade on special occasions, with a pipe in his mouth and a range of medals pinned to a military sash that was draped over his body.

He was a very intelligent dog and would know exactly what formation the different parades demanded.

In fact he was so intelligent that he could open and close doors on command and even fetch the daily newspaper from the post-box. Sergeant-Major De Beer had called him *Lelik* which in Afrikaans means ugly, and is pronounced *leer-luck,* although the *lik* is difficult to say with an English tongue.

Lelik didn't seem to mind at all. And even though he held high status in the family, and on the parade-ground itself, he was not necessarily a dog *vol fiemies* - full of airs, and fussiness.

Each winter he was quite content to travel to the De Beer farm in the Free State, some eight hundred kilometres from their home in Wynberg, in the boot of the family car. It was always something that amazed me as a little boy, that a dog was happy in the trunk of a car.

"Hi!" said Sharon. "Say hello to Sparky!"

Sparky, a Labradoodle, which is a cross between a Labrador and a Poodle, might have been even bigger than Lelik, but I was soon to find out that he had very few characteristics of the dog on the parade ground, of a military base.

As soon as the car stopped, he jumped out straight into a puddle in the gutter. He then came bounding over to me to say hello.

I am unsure if it was the smell of the chemicals I used to clean my velskoen, or the brand new jeans, but he went *befok* - crazy - when he reached me.

He danced up and down wildly, his legs pounding the ground, and with careful aim, it seemed, he planted his dirty paws onto my clean velskoen, soiling them immediately.

He proceeded to nudge whatever he thought he could find in my groin with his nose, so that I felt my body being lifting off the driveway itself.

Then he noticed my brand new jeans.

If indeed it was the smell of the new jeans, it set him off in a spasm of further exhibitionism, and something came over him suddenly. It was almost as if some spirit that was not necessarily *holy* had taken control of him.

He flung his front paws around my one leg and proceeded to copulate so aggressively I thought he would have a heart attack. I was certain that I would fall over, and very uncharacteristically I began to shout out in desperation.

"Oh, Sparky, *really!*" said Sharon.

But she said this as if the dog had brought over a toy for her to play with while she was busy making supper.

I did not think that this gentle approach would have much effect, so instead I began swearing loudly at him in Afrikaans, using as many unspeakable words as I could muster.

To be honest, I thought the dog was demented, and was probably having a fit.

I don't know whether suddenly he realised that, like him, I was also male or that he heard the tone of my voice, because he stopped and jumped right back onto the front seat.

"So," said Sharon. "You're ready for a ride down the strip, then?"

I tried my best to brush my soiled jeans, but was reluctant to wipe my velskoene, because they were made of skin, and any dirt could be embedded with such a wipe.

Sharon got into the driver's seat.

Sparky wouldn't budge.

"You'll enjoy it in the back," said Sharon, leaning over.

Clearly I had no choice.

I climbed in by sliding my butt over the side of the car so as not to disturb or entice Sparky by opening the passenger door. He was getting excited and started barking.

"I'm going to ride all the way down to East Beach, then come back along the strip to West Beach, go up the hill, turn around, and then we can go for dinner," said Sharon, as she started the car.

I decided to remain as quiet as possible just in case anything I had to say got Sparky going again.

As we drove east towards the end of White Rock, I settled down low in the back seat, hoping that neither Gord nor Johan could see me if they were sitting anywhere along the strip.

Each time someone waved or called out, Sparky barked back at them.

"Whooo-eee!" said Sharon, as a breeze caught the scarf she was wearing around her head.

I thought she looked just like Susan Sarandon in Thelma and Louise.

Every now and then she would give us a burst of speed and I found myself thrown into the back of the seat. I wondered whether it might be a good idea to remind Sharon of the speed limit in White Rock.

But then I thought of the time I had failed my learner's licence examination, and thought better of it.

Mindful of the fact that I came from a different culture, I had learnt here in Canada not to assume too much. But there have been times when I have not fully appreciated the differences, and such a time was when I attempted to answer some multiple choice questions at the ICBC licensing centre in Surrey.

I felt I was doing rather well, until I encountered this question:

You are driving in the passenger seat of a vehicle, and the driver is exceeding the speed limit.

Do you ...
- *pull the keys out of the ignition in order to bring the vehicle to a stop;*
- *raise your voice at the driver in order to cause*

> *alarm;*
- *ask whether the driver noticed the speed limit a few kilometres back;*
- *say that you're feeling uncomfortable with the speed of the vehicle?*

Clearly numbers one and two were wrong. That was easy. I liked number four but somehow it felt a little too touchy-feely. Number three on the other hand looked more objective and business-like.

I had gone for number three.

I failed the test.

When I asked a friend about this, he had looked at me and said, "Of course it's number 4. It's all about feelings here."

Now sitting in the back of Sharon's beautiful Bel Air I decided that I would not share my feelings about the speed limit along the strip, or anywhere else.

I felt that the signs posted along the way were clear enough.

Unfortunately, on our return, travelling due west, Johan noticed me in the back of the car.

He was sitting having a drink with his *tjerrie* (girl-friend) and watching the parade of vehicles.

"Hey! Jou moegoe, het jy iets gedoen? Hoekom sit jy agter?"

Moegoe is a name we, in South Africa, use to call someone who has done something silly. He wanted to know if I had done something wrong because I was sitting in the back of the car, rather than in the front.

I thought it was very unfair, and that he should rather be calling Sparky a *moegoe*, and not me.

I was so embarrassed that I slunk down as far as I could until my baseball cap fell off.

But when we reached the end of the strip on West Beach, I realised that I should rather have been paying closer attention to what was happening up front.

But not necessarily with Sparky, the dog.

I thought maybe it was time to adopt the Canadian way of doing things and say that I was *feeling uncomfortable*. Better still, I might have just said simply that she was driving too fast.

Sharon must have become bored with sticking to the speed limit. After all, she came from Abbotsford where they had a race track.

They even had an airport they claimed was *international*. I think this was just because some of their planes flew three kilometres over the border, into America.

Now I have heard it said that people have cars that emulate them and, also, sometimes that pets choose their owners and grow to be like them.

I don't know if this is true.

But when Sharon came to the end of West Beach and she noticed a steep hill, she went as *befok* as Sparky.

She put her foot down on that pedal so hard, I thought the end of the world had come, and The Beast himself was about to appear.

It reminded me of Blikkies Adonis, when I was young.

We used to call him Blikkies, which means *Tin*, because whenever we saw him with a tin in his hand, we knew for sure that there was some alcohol inside.

And he always seemed to be carrying a tin.

He was fired more times, from various jobs, than he had years in his date of birth, because people said he was too slow, and he could get nothing done.

Besides, he was always drunk.

But there was something remarkable about Blikkies. When he was sitting quietly, on some bench, and a young *meid* walked by, no matter how drunk he was, he would jump up like a pouncing leopard, in order to chat her up.

It was as though her sweet perfume did something deep inside his brain, because it never ceased to amaze us all just how fast he could launch that slow body of his into the air.

He would lurch forward so fast, it was as if he had some springboard underneath him. And when he followed that girl, he walked as though he had a steel brace in his back so upright was he, even though he did the walk *with* just the tiniest little swagger, as well.

And he would always say the same thing, no matter how many girls walked passed: *"Hello, my dah-ling. Kan ek 'n entjie saam met djo loep?"* Can I walk a little way with you?

I am sure that Bel Air must have been locked up in a garage for a long time, because when the fuel nozzle opened up wide in that carburettor, and injected the sweet-smelling high-octane gas into the combustion chamber, that engine came to life like a thoroughbred out of a starting gate.

Man! That Bel Air leapt forward, not unlike Blikkies going after a *tjerrie*, and with such a roar I imagined it must have rattled half the old age homes in White

Rock.

I fell deeper into the seat and was unable to see much at all, least of all the traffic signs warning drivers about the speed limit.

I am sure Sharon did not see them either.

Now, I perhaps need to remind you that Canada is not like South Africa in some ways, thankfully. In South Africa, drivers speed up when it rains and when they see a blind-rise ahead, they change down into a lower gear, put their foot down and overtake whatever is in front of them.

It takes balls to live there, and drive on the roads.

Canada, as I have said, is a gentle, slow-moving place.

And none more so than White Rock itself, with its speed limit of just 30 km/h down the strip on Marine Drive, beside the majestic Semiahmoo Bay.

Not even Australia drives that slowly.

There are times when I find myself a little more South African than Canadian, and I feel I could jump out of a car on Marine Drive, and run even faster.

Even in my sixties.

But when that Bel Air took off, I decided it was time to be a lot more Canadian than South African, and I began to moan loudly, in a desperate attempt to get in touch with my own feelings, on the back seat of that thrusting beast.

Sparky must have heard my moaning.

He turned around, took one look at me lying there and thought this was an invitation to play.

He landed right on top of me.

Suddenly, I heard a very loud, and ominous *BWOW-*

WOW-WOW!

I scrambled out from underneath Sparky, groping for my Canucks baseball cap.

There, right behind us, was a police car and a frantic-looking policewoman waving Sharon down.

Thankfully Sharon pulled over.

I said I thought she should switch the engine off.

She did.

Clearly her Bel Air did not like this.

The car began to shudder and shake as if starving for that sweet-smelling fuel. It was not unlike Blikkies Adonis's swagger when following a young girl on the street.

I climbed out, over the side, and stood in the road.

Still she shuddered and shook beside me.

And looking at her beautiful lines as I watched her shake like that, I realised there and then what Merle meant when she said the *spirit* came over her. And there was no doubt this was happening multiple times.

I shook my head, and came back to reality.

The policewoman was standing next to me.

"Good afternoon," she said, leaning over towards Sharon. "We were going a little fast I see. Out for an afternoon's drive?"

Sparky took one look at her.

He jumped from the back seat, right out of the car and into the street.

I fell to the ground and put my hands over my head, hoping rather that she would arrest me than endure another attack from the dog.

I don't know whether Sparky felt the need to make

amends for his homosexual encounter with me earlier, but when he saw the policewoman's trousers it was as if a mightily evil spirit got hold of *him*.

He jumped right onto both her legs, with such gusto I imagined he must have thought he was swinging from some chandelier also.

And he humped that poor policewoman's leg with such vigour, she began to cry out.

In fact he must have felt so taken with this new opportunity, he actually began to howl.

As I lay on the ground, all I could hear were the screams of the policewoman, and a quiet, calm voice of Sharon saying: "Oh Sparky, *really!*"

I was so confused, lying there in the street, that I could not decide what approach to take - one that was good for Canada, or perhaps another that worked better in South Africa.

But when I heard that women screaming, I realised that I needed to do something.

If it took balls to drive on the roads in South Africa, it would take even bigger ones to deal with this situation.

Thankfully, I think some spirit finally got hold of *me*.

I leapt up off the ground, dived over Sharon, pulled the keys from the ignition, grabbed hold of Sparky, dragged him to the back of the car. I opened the trunk, lifted him over the sill, put him inside and slammed the trunk shut.

There was, what seemed to be, a very long moment of silence.

The policewomen straightened her trousers, pulled

herself together, and bent down over the side of the Bel Air that had now only just stopped shaking.

I leant against the back of the car, wondering whether in the days to come I would be getting a visit from a White Rock by-law officer about cruelty to dogs.

As I said, they are gentle here in Canada, and I imagined that putting a dog in the trunk of a car would attract some attention.

But, when the policewoman had finished with Sharon, leaving her with a handful of tickets, Sharon beckoned me into the passenger seat and we drove back the one kilometre to my driveway.

With Sparky still in the trunk.

When we arrived at my house, Sharon got out of the Bel Air, walked to the back of the car and opened the trunk.

It was the most amazing thing - there lay Sparky, as calm as a lap dog on the couch watching a hockey game.

He raised his head, just a little, as if to say, *really, what do you want now?* And then he put his head down on the soft carpet of the truck of that beautiful red and white Bel Air.

Sharon climbed back into the driver's seat, waved goodbye, and drove off into the red sunset with the different coloured tickets stuck in her visor, and flapping in the breeze.

I saw her only once again.

I was driving down to Seattle one weekend with my *Little Angel*, for a getaway weekend.

We were listening to some Led Zeppelin - it might

even have been *Ramble On.*

I think Sharon was flying across the border in her Bel Air, on a getaway weekend of her own.

I was driving unlike a South African - very serenely, and in the slow, right-hand lane when Sharon passed us in her red and white Bel Air.

She was alone in the front of the car.

As she drove by us, with her scarf flowing in the wind, I remembered that she had said to me while driving down the strip in White Rock that day, that she never, *ever* went anywhere without Sparky.

When I saw a very large suitcase on the back seat of the car, it was then that I realised Sparky had found his place.

His fit.

Without the frenzied desire to go so *befok*, he must have been lying peacefully in the trunk of that beautiful Bel Air, on their journey to some international destination.

And for some reason, I found myself wondering if, back home, Blikkies ever got to find his own fit somewhere too, with some *lekker tjerrie*.

Perhaps he had finally succeeded and she, too, had a scarf that blew in the breeze as they walked down the road together.

Perhaps even to some international destination themselves, who knows?

6

When The Trains Roll By

Every man has an iconic male who plays the part of a role model.

Driver Du Toit was one of them, for me.

It is strange, but even in a bad society, sometimes good things happen. It was because I met Driver Du Toit that I met Patrick, and because I met Patrick that I met Merle and she then started working for my parents and became a member of our family.

And if the Universe makes connections, no connection could possibly be more strange than the fact that Gord, from the sauna, looked almost identical to driver Du Toit.

But it is perhaps unnecessary to look for so many co-incidences. What is important is that Driver Du Toit made an impression on me, and I on him.

I had just finished two years of conscription in our national service and I had some time on my hands. A friend had told me that getting a job as a fireman on a steam engine paid really good money.

And so it was that I found myself working with Driver Du Toit, on his steam engine, in the middle of the seventies when South Africa still had a large fleet of them in operation, and people would come from all over the world to photograph them. And us.

You might be wondering what this has to do with living in White Rock, British Columbia and dating. But in fact it is impossible to live in this small town and avoid the trains, and not see my Driver Du Toit. I see him regularly, high up on his seat, commanding the engine. Looking out over the tracks up ahead.

Looking out for any danger.

Leila found me online, and messaged me out of the blue one day.

She was obsessed with trains.

And in White Rock, it is impossible to avoid the trains. For some reason, the British Columbian government, or the little city of White Rock itself, had seen fit, many years before, to actually sell all of its water frontage to a foreign company in America in order to lay down tracks and have trains pass through.

I felt it was strange because I had never heard of a country selling sovereign land to a private company, and in another country. I had been used to 99-year leases in South Africa, as my father had once explained to me how they worked.

And so years later, in contrast to the small logging trains and a few others that brought tourists to the sleepy town of White Rock many years before, trains were now much longer, with not just one engine pulling them, but four, and each weighing hundreds of tonnes. And the fully loaded cargo trains weighed in more than the largest ferry in the British Columbian Ferry Services fleet.

And there are many of them each day, swamping the town itself. As you can imagine, many people are not impressed with these trains as they often wake the residents when blasting their horns early each morning. And the tracks, sadly, do a good job of separating the shoreline and the bay from the town itself.

Their presence presented a conflict inside of me, because I remembered Driver Du Toit with each one, and when a train goes by, I look up and honour my memory of him by acknowledging the driver himself. With at least a nod or a smile.

Of course there were some residents who glare at me, and one day one even said, "Don't wave at them, please; it only encourages them. We don't want the trains here."

Leila was different.

She became so excited when any train rumbled by, she would whistle, call out hooray! and sometimes jump up and down like a schoolgirl trying to attract the attention of the captain of her sporting team.

I asked her if her father had perhaps been an engineer, or what we in South Africa called a *drywer* in Afrikaans - a driver.

She said no. She simply loved trains.

I did not particularly like sarcasm, but I do remember saying to her, on that first meeting-date, that I felt she had come to the right place.

Because in White Rock, it is impossible to separate

oneself from the trains. The little city is only 3.5 square kilometres, and its waterfront promenade is only about 2,5 kilometres long. In most cases the trains themselves run the full length of this promenade.

Much to the delight of Leila.

And so it was that the three meeting-dates we enjoyed before the abrupt ending, consisted of her waving frantically at the engineers on board, and whooping with delight at the passing of each railcar.

I did relate a few details of our first meeting to Gord.

Uncharacteristically, he looked sideways at me. "If they like trains, it's probably because they come from some small town, or a farm, on the prairies. They're good people."

I nodded. Who could question Gord?

He was so certain about his observation that he added, "In fact, often the best kind of women."

Perhaps I felt we might have had a future, or perhaps I just wanted to impress Leila, but on our second date I mentioned that I had once derailed an entire train.

When she looked at me and whooped again, I was reminded of how that angel came to life in the stadium on Robben Island that night. It was as if I had flicked a switch and Leila lit up inside. Perhaps it was more appropriate to say that she looked almost as if she was going to explode.

"You derailed a whole train!" she shouted, getting up off the bench and responding so loudly, the people walking by stopped.

One even clapped.

I tried to look the other way, but could not escape this reaction that brought so much attention to both of us.

Thankfully, as Leila continued to shout, scream and holler with delight, another train came by and all but drowned her exuberance.

"Man!" said Leila when she finally sat down with the passing of the last railcar, "That must have been so awesome for you! I mean, what happened?"

I said that if she agreed to sit down with me at a coffee shop somewhere far from the thundering trains, I would tell her. I also suggested that she not become too excited with the unfolding of my story, as it was not that much of a spectacular derailment.

Just an ordinary one.

She agreed.

Once we reached the coffee shop, I settled down with a green tea latte and began.

Leila had decided on just a glass of water, and was eagerly waiting for the episode to unfold.

I told her that I was just nineteen, before I went to study to be a teacher. I had six months on my hands and someone persuaded me to join the railways as a stoker. They were also referred to as fireman.

During the interview, I thought this might mean that I was going to be putting fires out, but on my first day, I realised that I would actually be making them.

Leila's eyes opened wide.

I told her that I had reported for duty on a June morning, in the middle of winter, at 05:45, to Salt River Depot in Cape Town, to be greeted by long lines of steam engines.

Large ones, small ones, dirty ones and others that looked as though they had just been delivered from some showroom because, lovingly tended to by their drivers, they gleamed with the gold reflection of their highly polished brass in the early morning light, and their shining black boilers.

It was a frightening moment for me - dark, raining and very cold.

I didn't think, I told Leila, that I had any idea what I had let myself in for.

I had clutched, in one hand, a small box of food and a drink I had been told to prepare for myself. And in the other a small bag with pyjamas and a change of clothing. We were going over the pass, sleeping at a siding overnight, and coming back the following day.

As I walked over the tracks looking for my engine, and Driver Du Toit, I suddenly realised that I might have let myself in for something that was a little beyond me. Drivers and firemen stared at me. Some making comments about the new rookie. A few shaking their heads; clearly they knew what I was about to discover.

The engines themselves spewed out steam, oil, water; they heaved and coughed as though they were alive, even though still stationary there in the yard, their drivers tending to them, oiling them down one side, and then down the other. It was as if they did this with love. And with each oiling, with each touch, the engines themselves seemed to sigh or groan gently in response.

It was an eerie scene, I told Leila. And that first day I would not ever forget.

I could see the fireman on the footplates above me, cleaning the interior, and now and then throwing a shovel-full of coal into the red hot furnace.

I continued to walk over each track. I felt that I might never be able to do what was expected of me.

But then a large man, holding an oilcan, raised his hand and greeted me. He called my name. It was Driver Du Toit.

"Good morning," he said. "Report to Nico up there," he pointed to the cabin itself.

I nodded. I climbed up.

It was hot inside.

Nico greeted me and showed me where to put my bag.

"You keep out of my way, and just watch. Don't try to do anything. After a few days I will start telling you what I am doing. But for the first few days, just watch."

I nodded.

I was dressed in work pants, boots, and a dark shirt. I could feel the heat of the fire on them.

Driver Du Toit climbed up, shook my hand and sat down.

"So you're here with us for six weeks. To learn."

I nodded.

"And then the exam?"

I nodded.

"I will give you one of my books I used to learn the rules of the road, with drawings of all the signs. You will learn from it, look after it and give it back to me when you have finished the exam."

I nodded.

He settled down. A shunter came up to the side of the cabin, below. For a while they talked. I was to learn, soon, that it was the shunter's job to make sure the train had the right railcars.

And this later became really important with the derailment, I told Leila.

She exclaimed with a soft whimper.

I thought about asking her if she had ever seen or travelled with a steam engine, but I decided against it.

I resumed my story about that first day.

It was time to go, I told her.

"Gooi!" Driver Du Toit beckoned to Nico. Throw!

I turned to look at the fire doors. On the boiler in front of me was a nameplate in shining brass - details of the model and manufacturer.

It also read, two fireman every eight hours.

Nico saw me staring at it.

He smiled.

"Don't wait for anyone else..."

And he began to throw coal. Lots of it.

After what seemed like a very long time, he stopped, sat down and lit a cigarette.

He and Driver Du Toit were looking up at the steam gauge. It was close to the red-line they were waiting for.

Just before it reached the red-line, Driver Du Toit pushed the large accelerator down towards the fire doors.

The engine groaned, all four pistons working as if with immense primordial effort. And then a skid-shudder, as one wheel slipped. And then another.

But with each sshhoef! of steam, and forward

thrust of the pistons themselves I could sense the engine trying desperately to bite into the track in its quest for true, lasting traction.

Then, suddenly, we were moving.

And as we pulled out of the yard, she couldn't help herself, and let go. And the steam valve opened wide, and it felt as though the entire engine exploded. The steam came pouring out above us so loudly I thought it would wake the city itself.

But it did not last long, and soon we were chugging down the line, eastwards, towards the Hottentots Holland mountains, and Sir Lowry's Pass itself.

I said to Leila that I knew we were going to go through the tunnel in the mountain and come out on the other side.

Nico didn't manage to sit down for very long, to rest and to smoke his cigarette.

With just a flick of Driver Du Toit's left hand, he would slide off his seat and start shovelling the coal from the tender behind us, into the hungry fire.

Every time Driver Du Toit opened the doors, Nico's swing was perfect, and into the furnace the coal flew, thudding against the sides of the boiler walls, or its roof.

And then the doors were closed again, and the burning on my pants, against my skin stopped. But only for the few seconds it took Nico to turn around, pick up another shovel-full and thrust it, forward, into the flames beyond the open door.

Leila looked as though she needed to take a deep breath.

I took a sip of my green tea. And then continued.

I told her that once I had counted how many shovelfulls of coal Nico threw before we left the yard.

Leila stared at me. I asked her how many she thought he would have to throw before Driver Du Toit decided it was enough to start our journey.

"I...I don't know! Fifty?"

I told her that once I had counted two hundred and fifty five throws. And each shovelful weighed around fourteen pounds, or seven kilograms.

"That's a lot of coal," said Leila, "a lot of coal!"

I remember Nico sitting down with his cigarette, and within minutes, Driver Du Toit beckoning with his hand. And the process would start all over again.

When we got to the tunnel, things got scary, I told her.

Leila sat there with her mouth slightly open. I could see she was in great suspense.

"The tunnel? What happened?"

I shook my head, adding slightly to the drama of the story itself.

Just before we entered, I told her, I could see Driver Du Toit looking up at the steam gauge. He saw me notice his glance, and he commented:

"We must make sure there is enough steam to get us through the tunnel. If there is not enough, we're in trouble..."

Leila held her hand up against her mouth. "What did he mean by that...?"

Well, I explained to her, as though I were an expert on trains, which I knew I was not. If there was not enough steam, the steam-brakes would come on automatically. And if that happened in the middle of the tunnel, there are only two things the fireman can do.

Leila leant forward. "Throw more coal to make more steam!"

Well, I told her, cocking my head to one side - this is true.

But the problem with this option is that more coal makes more smoke. And smoke inside a tunnel is not a good idea.

Leila looked a little frantic.

"But they can crawl out, right? I mean, there must be space between the engine and the tunnel wall..."

I nodded slowly. But then, shook my head also. Slowly. And in deference.

I told her I could well remember the sad look on Driver Du Toit's face when he told me how his nephew had died inside that tunnel.

Leila gasped.

"Hy was te vet," he had said, looking at me, assuming I understood. He was too fat.

I told her I had put two and two together, and realised that he could not fit between the engine and the wall of the tunnel itself.

He had suffocated, desperately trying to build up more steam, while the driver himself had escaped.

Leila gasped.

In fact it was such a gasp that it reminded me of the sound when the fireman kicked the lever on the footplate of the cabin, expertly working it back and forth with the toe of his boot, so as to create a vacuum, and thereby the suction needed so the water could flow from the tender behind us into the boiler.

I could remember how it had taken me four or five attempts before I was able to do this. The first few had resulted in a rush of steam down the side of the engine itself, almost connecting with an angry shunter who was coming up beside us, and water gushing out of the pipe below, onto the tracks.

Nico had laughed at me.

But when I got it right, the gasp of that sound make me think, there on the footplate inside the cabin, that with the hissing of steam and the engine's gentle grumbling and groaning, that I was attending to a living thing.

And any engine was always a female to all of us.

And I told Leila that the precise nudge of that short water lever, this way and that, on the floor of the footplate reminded me how much those gentle proddings made her truly come alive, as if it was just what she had been waiting for. How the right touch could, in fact, make her groan from pure satisfaction - like when that water began to flow through her and the water level began to rise in the glass, she always seemed to make a deep sigh.

I noticed Nico smiled each time. And after a while, I smiled too.

I told Leila I felt this was a mystery, because deep down, I knew the engine was just a machine. Even though it was not what I experienced each day I was on any steam engine. There was always some realisation, some feeling that I was wrong about this. And it was a feeling that haunted me.

Just that little kick, a nudge - a touch, and she seemed to calm down. Each time.

I don't think Leila blinked once.

In fact, I became so concerned, that I stopped with my story, and got up to fetch her another glass of water.

When I returned it was as if she, too, had calmed and when I sat down again she said, "I can see it. I can almost smell that fire, and see the water rise in her boiler. Please don't stop..."

I was starting to become concerned, and wondered whether we should rather change the venue and go somewhere private.

I was worried that when I reached the climax of the story, Leila might become so excited, she too might blow off some steam, right there in the coffee shop, and in front of other people.

I did not in any way want to have the kind of reputation that I was someone who set dates on fire.

But then I remembered this was only our second meeting, and that suggestions of such things, like a private location were not proper, and I might very easily lose any further opportunity to see her again. And so I continued with my story.

I told her that we made it through the tunnel, with the steam gauge not far from the red-line mark, and when we reached the summit and levelled out, she let go again, and spewed her heat and the contents of her belly out through that escape valve stirring the rocks, and the fynbos - heather - that blew gently in the breeze on top of the mountain itself.

Leila stared dead ahead, at me.

I told her we had a good night's sleep. And the next morning took on coal and water, and collected the long train of apples at the Elgin siding, and started our way back down the mountain.

I stopped talking for a moment, and made as though I was stirring my cup of latte that was now empty.

Leila could see that something might be wrong and she touched my hand. "Did something go wrong?"

I told her that it was a difficult memory, but that nothing had gone wrong that particular day. Although, thinking about it again, I realised that day was the start of it.

In fact we made it to the bottom of the mountain, through the tunnel. We had stopped at Sir Lowry's Pass Village station to take on a little more water. To visit the little shop on the platform, and buy some cigarettes. I can remember buying a large, cold Coke and another packet of Chesterfield Mild. Nico had bought a packet of Lucky Strike. Plain.

Driver Du Toit was nervous, in his seat, high up in the cabin.

We knew that this village had a bad reputation for riots, insurrections, mobbings and general social unrest.

It was in the middle of apartheid, and three white men stopping, albeit inside a large engine on the tracks, attracted attention. No one knew why this village was so traumatised; perhaps it was because it was so far from any major centre. Perhaps the small police station was under-staffed. All I learnt that day was that it was an unsafe place, and if there were riots in Cape Town, they would always somehow start there.

Driver Du Toit called us. "Kom, ons moet ry!" Come, we must go.

Nico and I climbed back up into the cabin.

"So you made it back to Cape Town?" said Leila.

I thought about it, looking down at my empty mug, and realised that my memory was fading - it was such a long time ago that I could not remember whether it was that trip, or another, that saw Nico and me inside the coal tender behind us.

It could not have been that day, because I remember taking coal at Elgin. The tender must have been full.

Perhaps it was another time. But I told Leila there, inside that coffee shop, how one day Nico and I, some five or six kilometres from Salt River Depot, had run out of coal. The gauge was dropping. Thankfully we did not have a full load behind us, but we could not stop in the middle of the main track.

It would have been embarrassing.

Driver Du Toit laughed, and pointed to a little cupboard under Nico's seat.

Nico opened it and took out a small dust pan and two brushes.

He beckoned to me, and we both climbed into that coal tender and gathered the last remaining coal dust to get our engine and our train back into the depot. I had, at first, burst out laughing at him, thinking it was a joke.

But I shall never forget standing upright in that tender that day. I looked around and realised that Nico had, single-handedly, thrown some fourteen tonnes of coal from the time we had left our siding many hours before.

"That's a lot of coal!" gasped Leila. "Fourteen tonnes - oh, my God!"

I got up and filled her glass with water. The bubbles gurgled inside the large container on top of the counter as the fresh cold water came spewing out the bottom.

Leila beckoned to me, her hand up in the air, "I need a coffee. I can just feel it - the derailment is coming up..."

I watched her approach the counter. I felt a little uncertain. Should I be letting go of all this on just our second meeting-date, I thought? What more would I have to tell her, I felt, if I told her everything right there?

She sat down again.

"So you said that the driver was responsible for the engine. And the....the shunter was responsible for the railcars. I know that this is important when it comes to the derailment, right?"

I nodded.

That particular night, I told her, I had been driving the train. But it was all about the shunter.

In fact it was Patrick. A brand new shunter on our watch.

I told Leila that we had to go forward a couple of months.

I had studied driver Du Toit's book from cover to cover. And I had passed the two-hour oral exam.

When I came for my last shift with driver Du Toit and Nico, I had climbed up onto the footplate, and there was my driver beaming from ear to ear.

"They told me you got a distinction. I have never had a fireman who got a distinction. You make me proud man. You make me proud," said driver Du Toit.

And so it was that I never forgot driver Du Toit's teaching. And his pride when I had made the grade.

But it was his patience, above all else, that I remembered. How he worked his engines, how he fed them the oil from his personal oil can each time, as though he was tending to something he loved. And how he had treated both of us. Never shouting, even when we made a mistake.

He had been a true gentleman.

I stopped briefly, and I must have had a tear in my one eye, because Leila reached out and touched my cheek. Her head was bent to one side and she looked sad.

"I know something happened," she said. "It's okay. You can tell me about it."

I shook my head, wiped my eyes and said that I had promised to tell her about the derailment, and that was what I was going to do.

After I said goodbye to driver Du Toit, they posted me to the harbour of Cape Town, I told her.

Thankfully I had a much smaller engine - an S-class, if I remember. She was a shunting engine, I said. It never went *op die pad* - on the road as we called it. Instead she scuttled between all the warehouses, connecting long trains, positioning them, and making them ready for the larger engines to collect them the next day, or that evening, depending on the shift, for the long journey up country.

And thankfully unlike Nico's engine, she carried

only three tonnes of coal.

I had a very different driver. He was much younger. A tough man who was very much unlike Driver Du Toit.

But we did also have some fun.

Our favourite thing was to drag-race that small S-Class engine down along a straight track in the shunting yard.

One time he challenged me, betting me two Rands, which was the price of a restaurant meal in those days, that he could out-accelerate me in my Volkswagen Beetle.

Leila's jaw dropped.

"And what happened?"

I told her that to my own amazement, over about one hundred metres or so, he managed to do just that, and from a standstill.

They were perky little engines, those S-Classes.

Patrick was the shunter who was assigned to us most nights, and by this time he and I were friends.

He was Coloured and it was, I told Leila, only in 1975 that the South African Railways & Harbours employed non-white people to such an important job for the first time.

He came aboard at the start of each shift, and chatted to both my driver, and to me.

Nico, in the four-piston Garratt engine had taught me how to cook bacon and eggs, and *boerewors* - sausage - using the shovel as a frying pan and the heat of the fire inside the fire-box as an oven.

We had many delicious meals that way.

When I was posted to the harbour shunting yard,

and met Patrick, I used to cook for all of us. And I think this is how Patrick and I became friends.

And then he had introduced Merle to me. And it was a blessing, because my parents were looking for a housekeeper. I told Leila that Merle had been with them ever since. Even when she was semi-retired, she still did work for them because my mother said she was family and she could not imagine life without her.

Anyway, our normal night shift, in the harbour, consisted of us arriving at around six in the evening.

Patrick would come and fetch us, and give my driver some idea of how much shunting we would be doing that night.

In most cases, we were done by around ten o'clock. And my driver would pull up between two buildings, out of the way and out of sight. And he would take the shovel, and expertly throw just enough coal onto the fire, almost blackening the red surface, so that very little glow was visible. He would fill the boiler with water, and then settle down for the rest of the night, and sleep.

When Patrick came to fetch us the next morning around five o'clock, the fire would be glowing perfectly, the water half way down and we would make the slow journey back to the yard, clean up and go off shift.

But this one night it was different, I said.

Leila leant forward again, her eyes slightly wider.

Patrick kept coming back, I told her.

It was this track, then another, this train, then another. So many railcars had to be coupled to so many different trains on different tracks that long after midnight my driver became irritated.

I didn't like the look of his eyes when he was angry.

And I had seen him angry now and then, like when I had levelled the coal inside the firebox with the long fire-iron.

I never found out what that fire-iron was meant for, but when he saw me using it to level the coals inside the firebox he was enraged. He said that if he caught me levelling the fire with that fire-iron again, he could *bliksem* me - beat me - so that I would never be able to throw coal again.

He told me a good fireman throws the coal right. And that is how a fire is level - by throwing coals properly. Not with anything else, least of all a fire-iron.

After that day I was a little scared of him.

And it was a weird thing, but years later when I heard about Driver Du Toit, I also heard about that driver whose name I will not mention in case his family is still around, and alive. But, I told Leila, he had gotten into some altercation at home, and had murdered his uncle.

I never levelled the coals with anything ever again.

He was a naughty man, too, and used to spend most of his days out on the road, on his bike, looking for young girls.

Clearly he relied on his night's sleep in the cabin of his S-Class engine to catch up.

But that night there was no catching up.

We were busy doing one *afskop* after the other.

This was an illegal manoeuvre that most drivers in shunting yards agreed to do.

It entailed shunting a long train towards, and over

a junction point. The shunter would swivel a green light, signalling that he wanted us to accelerate, and then just before the junction itself, he would switch to a red light, signalling us to stop as quickly as possible.

He would have already uncoupled the railcar at the end, and that would then continue to travel down the track to join the particular train it was assigned to.

This, I told Leila, was called a flying shunt - *afskop*, or in direct translation, a kick-off.

It was illegal, because many manoeuvres took place at high speed, and some railcars contained animals or dangerous chemicals. I must admit that most drivers would not do it when this was the case.

One flying shunt actually involved Patrick one day, I told Leila. I was smiling when I said this, because it was so funny.

We always had what north Americans call a caboose. It was a small railcar that housed guards or personnel that travelled with a train, usually on long journeys. In fact we called it just a guard van.

There was always one at the back of every train.

One morning we were shunting, and my driver and I watched as another engine did flying shunts up and down on the track next to ours. Eventually the guard van had to be attached to the end of the train.

Patrick and another shunter got on board. Of course they were both new in the job.

The idea was that one shunter would look out of the window and call out to the other shunter to turn the wheel at the back of the guard van in order to apply the brake. The flying shunt was particularly fast and if they didn't apply the brake, the van could collide mightily with the rest of the train.

They flew past us, down the track, at high speed. Unfortunately the communication between Patrick and the other shunter had not been good, because as that guard van sped down the track on a collision course with the end of a very long train, each shouted to the other: "Draai! Draai die briek!" Turn, turn the brake!"

Neither of them could see it, but their heads, each stuck out of the opposite window meant that there was nobody turning any handbrake inside that guard van.

And, man, did that van hit that train with a force.

Its back wheels jumped straight up into the air, and it was a miracle that van did not end up on its side next to the train.

Both Patrick and the other shunter could be seen coming down the tracks towards us, each holding their heads in their hands and shouting obscenities at one another. *"Jou stupid fok! Ek't gesê draai die fokken briek!"* You stupid f*&#k, I told you to turn the brake!

Of course it didn't sound as funny in English.

Leila laughed, nevertheless.

Anyway, I continued, that night we did flying shunts, one after the other. The engine itself was at the end of a siding, so we were doing these shunts backwards.

Not that this mattered in any way.

I could see my driver becoming more irritable.

"Kan jy dryf?" he asked me at one point. Can you drive?

I was taken aback as this was a privileged and important job. I could not believe he was actually wanting me to drive the engine itself.

Leila squealed, softly.

I told her that I got up off my chair and walked to his side of the footplate.

I looked at the long accelerator on the left of his seat. And then at the gear lever that was either pushed forward in order to advance, or backwards in order to reverse.

I had also noticed that when he wanted to stop he would quickly pull the accelerator up towards him. Then immediately after that, push the gear lever in the opposite direction, and then pull down the steam brake so that it was horizontal. The engine would stop within a very short distance. This was essential so that the rest of the train, in a flying shunt, did not go over the points.

He got up off his seat.

I sat down where I had watched him sit all those months. It felt strange.

I took a deep breath.

The first time I touched the accelerator I was terrified. I had been attending to her, loving her, filling her with coal. With precious water. Looking after her just as Nico and driver Du Toit had taught me.

But touching her there, on that handle was quite another thing. It took me to a higher place. What if she didn't want to respond to me? What if she didn't like my touch, I thought.

I pushed the accelerator down, gently. We moved down the track, but too slowly, so he beckoned for me to push the long handle down further.

I did so. Soon we were moving effortlessly.

He watched my every move. Forward. Stop. And then back. Stop. Change gear. Flick the steam brake up to release it. Down, to activate it when I pulled the accelerator up, to stop. Then we moved in the opposite direction when I moved the gear lever forward.

He must have watched me for about ten minutes.

"Jy kan dryf," said finally. You can drive.

He went to my side of the cabin, and began to shovel coal into the firebox. He carefully filled the boiler with water. And then he did the most amazing thing. He settled down for the night and fell asleep.

"No!" said Leila, almost knocking her cup of coffee over.

I breathed in deeply, stirring the memories within me.

I told her that it was actually quite easy. I sat with my back to the open window, so I could lean out and look down the track. My left hand would normally have been positioned on the handle of the accelerator.

But because we were shunting backwards, I had my back to the window, and so I manoeuvred the accelerator with my right hand in fact.

And my right hand was also ready to instantly pull down the steam break, and also change the gear to either forward or reverse.

Because I knew, that if we were travelling forwards, I would be sitting facing forwards, and that my left hand would be working the long handle of the accelerator, and my right both the gear lever, and the steam brake, I took notice of the fact that my first driving position was different.

Leila had her mouth open again.

I told her I got so good, that after my third flying shunt I felt myself becoming confident.

My engine and I were working in unison, as though we were one.

And I told her it was just like...; but then I stopped and changed my mind. It was, I told her instead, like cooking a meal together with a woman, and laughing at the same things.

It was a thrill to be there in the middle of the night with her; alone.

To be in full control of this huge, beautiful beast that breathed; that was alive.

Even though, I reminded her, it was just an S-Class steam engine.

Leila took a quick sip of coffee, but soon realised her cup was empty, so she held up her hand and quickly filled it with fresh dark roast. Black. And when I looked down at her cup, I realised it was as black as those steam engines had been the first time I had laid eyes on them.

"Okay, go on," she said.

I tried to describe the darkness all around, in the dead of night. And the silence.

Except for the breathing of the engine: her gentle, slow hissing. Her sighs. And, now and then, the urgent gasps when I accelerated her, or the disappointed hisses when I slowed her down.

Or stopped her.

I felt, that night, that I learnt for the first time what it is to be connected to another life form. When I touched her there on her accelerator, enticing her to move, she always drew in a little breath, just before her wheels began to turn. It was an interaction that made me feel more authentic, more alive.

I leant out backwards, my head out of the window, and looked down the track.

Far in the distance, I could see Patrick, I said.

There was some movement on the side of the last railcar. He was uncoupling it.

And then, suddenly, the urgent sideways-flick of the his green lantern: *afskop* - kick-off!

I pulled the gear lever down towards me for reverse. Remember, I told Leila, we were shunting backwards.

I released the steam brake, pushing it up. And pushed the accelerator down, gently, towards the door of the firebox. And when she began to grip the tracks, down even further. Further, even more.

We were now going fast, rocking gently from side to side as we went down the long track itself.

It was what the engine did: rock, from side to side as she thrust herself forward. Or back.

And then, suddenly, it happened.

Leila could not contain herself. She let out a whimper.

I told her that the engine shuddered, shaking from side to side much more violently than usual.

I did not wait for the red lantern.

I instantly yanked the accelerator up. All the way, towards me.

I grabbed the gear lever and thrust it forward.

And as my hand came down I pulled, with urgency,

the steam brake into a horizontal position in front of me.

The jerking, the sudden de-acceleration, the quick squeal from her belly, and the groan she made as her wheels bit into those tracks woke my driver.

"Wat was dit?!" he shouted. What was that?!

I was terrified.

Leila grabbed my one arm. And then put her hand up against her mouth with her other hand.

I realised, I said to her, that something had gone terribly wrong.

My driver got up and looked out of the window. And then he climbed down from the engine, and walked along the tracks.

I knew I could not avoid taking a look myself.

Slowly, I leant out of the driver's window and peered into the darkness.

It was a sight to behold, I said to Leila who by now had tears in her eyes.

There were railcars everywhere, I told her.

They were spread all over the quayside. Scattered, carelessly, like dinky toys a little boy had thrown out into his back yard.

I paused, and then looked down at my empty mug of latte. I told Leila, I could feel my heart beating wildly when I saw all those railcars thrown around like that.

I asked Leila if she could remember what I had said about the driver, and that he was responsible for the engine alone.

She nodded, not able to say anything. Her one hand was now gripping my left arm so tightly I could feel the blood-flow stop.

I told her I had managed to stop our engine just three or four metres from the junction point itself.

Poor old Patrick had not switched the point fully - the railcars had all been empty and were therefore very light, I told her. One had jumped over the point itself and dragged all the others with it.

Leila gasped.

My driver came back to the cab. He looked up at me. *"Jy't goed gedoen. Die engine staan nog reg!"* You did well. The engine is fine.

Leila gasped again, letting go of my arm.

I flexed my fingers, and let the blood flow back again. It was almost painful.

I told her it took them just two hours to put those railcars back on the tracks.

I never drove a steam engine again after that night, but until my very last day, my driver always looked at me with more respect. And sometimes, he even gave me a smile.

I told Leila that it had been like being with a beautiful woman. And then something terrible had happened, and I was never allowed to be alone with her again. Even though, when I returned to just taking on water and feeding her coal, I never felt that she was in any way angry with me. It was just that I could never be with her in that special way again.

I think it was on that date that Leila held my hand very tightly as we walked from the coffee shop onto the promenade on Marine Drive.

We did meet once again.

But I am not sure I should say too much about that

third date. Perhaps I should be remembering it as our first proper date - but I think that the memory of that derailment became even clearer when we met again.

Leila made me repeat the entire episode, word for word and I shudder, just like that engine on the track that day, when I recall what happened as a result of my retelling the entire story, alone that night with her.

It reminded me so much of being alone, in the darkness, with that little S-Class.

And it made Leila's ending even more difficult for me, because that night I learned that knowing how and where to touch a woman can produce wonderful outcomes.

I did not see Leila again, because soon after that wonderful evening, she had gone jogging on the tracks and a train had struck her.

When they found her earphones ripped and torn to shreds, one earpiece on one side of the track, and the other on the other side, the police came to the conclusion that she had been listening to music, and so could not hear the honking of the train's horn.

And whenever I think of how much she had loved trains, it made me truly sad.

Because now, when I walk down the promenade, it is difficult to do so without thinking of her.

And I think, also, of my driver Du Toit.

He, sitting so high up on that driver's seat. And how good he had been to me.

It was many years later, just after Emma and I had married, that I saw Patrick again. It was, funnily enough in Adderley Street, just outside Die Groote Kerk - more of that later.

He told me they had killed Driver du Toit - *mors-dood*.

One evening he had stopped at Sir Lowry's Pass station, to take on water and feed his engine, just as we had done that first time I travelled with him into that dark tunnel, and through the mountain itself.

The people in the village had been rioting.

"Hulle het hom met 'n baksteen deur die venster doodgegooi," said Patrick, looking down. They threw a brick at him through the window and killed him.

They had then dragged him off from the footplate of his beloved engine, and beaten him until he was unrecognisable.

I was glad I had made him proud that day when I passed my exam with a distinction, and remember how he had bragged about me to the other drivers.

And so, when I walk along the tracks here in White Rock, and look up, and catch the eye of one of the engineers in a train, and wave, I think of my driver Du Toit, and of how he must have felt a premonition of his own death that day we had stopped at that station, all those years before.

Because I remember, so well, how he had been agitated that night and how he had urged us to climb back onto the engine, and to get going as quickly as possible.

And it makes me sad to think of him lying there on the ground, next to his mistress. And I wonder what gentle, mournful groaning that engine might have made there at that station, knowing that she would have to make the journey back home without him.

And I sometimes imagine that I know just how she

might have felt when I think of Leila. Because the day she died I realised I would never get to feel her exuberance, or hear her exclamation at the sight of a train ever again.

And, with her passing, I realised just how quiet it really is for me when the trains roll by.

7

Too Hot To Handle

It took me a few weeks before I returned to Gord and the sauna.

I saw him again when I felt I was perhaps ready to venture forward.

He asked me how things were going. I had no idea whether he had heard about Leila and I felt it best not to talk about her as I had struggled with her passing.

By this time Trevor's banning was over and he was lurking around the water fountain. In order to avoid any more unpleasantness, I enticed Gord into the sauna next door.

I could not remember having told him much about Sharon and Sparky, so I said that I felt it was a bit unfair he had not warned me about women with large dogs.

"I don't have any experience with women and large dogs," he said, after sitting down.

I had half a mind to tell him exactly what I thought,

but I felt that my experience in this regard might result in his not giving me any more advice, so I remained silent.

I could detect that something was wrong, however.

After a while I asked whether things were alright at home.

"I am thinking of moving to Kelowna. I have a cottage there, and I do love the skiing and the lake."

I nodded.

Kelowna is a city on a large lake. I had spent a weekend there before my beloved Emma had died. The lake itself is more than 180 kilometres long. I could only imagine the views from the hillside.

"My son says he doesn't really want to come with me," said Gord.

I suggested that he might not like the fresh water idea, or perhaps Kelowna itself, and that it was perhaps because he was a teenager that he was resisting.

I got a look from Gord.

"He's twenty-four. He never comes down from his room upstairs, so he wouldn't even know what a lake looks like."

I held back, knowing that I could offer no advice about stairs or lakes or enticing boys to do anything. Also because I knew that if I waited long enough Gord would volunteer more.

He did.

"He's upstairs on his computer all day, playing games."

I thought back to the time in 1982 when I flew a plane on a flight simulator with a Sinclair computer that had only 48Kb of RAM. I felt tempted to say that today, one page of typing would be far more than this, but I kept quiet.

Apart from this, I had little computer gaming experience and so decided that I had nothing to add.

We continued to sweat it out and in the heat of the moment I tried to imagine what Merle would say about this.

Stompie her son, whose nickname means *cigarette butt* on account of the fact that he was short and Urban legends had it that smoking stunted one's growth, had come home one day with wild stories. He had been talking with a *larney* (wealthy/yuppy) friend who clearly must have been working for some large overseas corporation.

Stompie began asking Merle about human rights, sick-leave and pensions.

When Merle reminded him that she had supported him until he decided to leave school, had then taught him the flower business, and mentored him until he was able to purchase a small home and a portable braai (barbeque), he became even more belligerent.

When he had become addicted to *tik* (a particularly vile form of crystal-meth) she said she had had enough, gave him a *snotklap* and threw him out of the house.

I had no intention of telling Gord this. It was just that these thoughts came flowing through my mind there in the sauna. In the heat of everything.

I was mindful of the fact that in Canada children could divorce their parents even if they just looked at them funny, and I was not about to reveal to Gord that according to the Urban Dictionary, a *snotklap* meant administering *a hard open-handed slap sufficient that it causes mucus that was formerly inside the recipient to come out rapidly.*

Merle had said this was called tough-love. Not just the snotklap, but kicking him out.

As we sweated further, I was glad that I had not volunteered this information, because it was a strange thing - as though he was reading my mind - suddenly he began with a long story that immediately alerted me to the danger of strong discipline of the type that Merle believed in.

"You remember that old couple that used to capture young girls, back East?"

I said I did not.

"Yeah. Well they used to cruise around and find them on the streets and take them out to their farm and murder them after keeping them for a while."

There was this one father who didn't like his daughter's boyfriend. She asked him if she could go to a party. He said yes, but then found out she had gone with the boyfriend. He was so angry about it, he locked her out of the house, when she came home."

Gord was silent for a short while. I anticipated a very bad ending, so I did not dare venture any comment. I was careful to not even breath too deeply.

"They found her three weeks later. Like it was something out of The Silence Of The Lambs."

I was shocked, especially considering that this movie was in my top ten. The very capturing of the girl in the film was copied from a book I had read called The Collector, by John Fowles.

But then I felt guilty, thinking about the book and

the movie, and I thought about that father.

I remembered a school friend of mine who had graduated as a psychiatrist. She had always said that the most brutal life experience was to outlive one's children.

I realised that in this case, if the story were true, this parent not only outlived his daughter, but had to also accept that he had perhaps caused her death. I shivered, even as the sweat poured down from my forehead onto the floor beneath me.

Perhaps it was not a good idea to suggest to Gord that he lock his son out of his house.

I considered relating this story to Merle, and that in Canada we don't do things this way.

But then I remembered the power with which she could deliver a *snotklap*, and I decided against it.

Gord exited to visit the water fountain and I continued to sit quietly and contemplate the trials and pains that Life sometimes presents.

Little did I know that a trial of my own was soon to reveal itself - it would not be as much as the pain I imagined Gord might feel if he should kick his son out, but nevertheless it was painful enough.

Gord returned looking a lot better, and sat his large frame down some distance from me.

"So you're done with dogs," he said.

This sounded like more of a statement than a question.

I said I was.

"You do know that women really like food," he said.

I was not sure what he meant. From the size of

some of them I could see that, but then again there were many women in Canada who were very trim.

I mentioned this to him.

"Yeah - that's something else you need to look out for - women who are too active - before you know it you'll be forking out thousands every winter to ski and snowboard. Then in summer they'll expect you to hike every mountain."

He ventured nothing further for a while and I found myself reminded of a profile I had read the weekend before, and which had gone something like this: *I am a happy and active person and although I can be found in an evening dress, I can also get going in other attire - I love hiking, kayaking, snowboarding, skiing, sailing, paragliding and reading. But don't get me wrong, I also enjoy a cuddle on the couch sometimes.*

Such profiles terrified me, as all I was able to muster each day was an hour's walk and a couple of lengths in the pool. In between visits to the sauna to get dating advice from Gord.

I had thought paddle-boarding would be easy because I had had a skateboard as a child, but it had ended in disaster when the paddleboard had deflated, far out in the bay.

It was an experience I shall not easily forget. I had promised myself, afterwards, I would never again complain about the over-cautious lifeguards at the pool as I had spent a good hour waving frantically, hoping that one of them might be walking on the shoreline with their date.

Hence, I subjected myself to the quarrels in the sauna as my only extreme sport.

Gord was still silent, so I continued to think of the women I had encountered that morning on Match.com, and thought about her *reading*.

I marvelled that she had any time for it. I decided, after going through the long list of sporting activities in my head, once again, that she must have all her books on a tablet or an iPad, and perhaps read them while she was skiing.

I wondered whether she did all these things in one day.

The *cuddle on the couch* appealed to me, but I imagined also that after all that activity she would fall asleep, just like Zoe.

Gord got a new wind suddenly.

"Don't forget about the food. They love a man who appreciates a good meal. There's a site called Epicurious.com - go find a good recipe and get the list of ingredients. Make sure they're fresh. That will impress them."

My head was spinning. Should I look for a woman who appreciated a man who liked food, or should I find a recipe and the ingredients first.

I asked Gord.

He did some of his strange breathing before he answered: "Get the recipe, and ingredients on a list. Every second women will have something about cooking in her profile."

I nodded.

He was right. Very few did not mention something about food. And I had also seen what might have been an appeal to connect with a man who appreciates cooking.

I found someone the next day.

Her name was Magdalene Paine. Although her handle was something like *loveisforeal112.*

When I found myself wondering what *foreal* meant, I realised that I was still very much of a novice.

She specifically mentioned that she liked to share good food, as much as she liked a cuddle on the couch and some intimacy.

Various themes were popping up all the time and I felt that the Universe was aligning me for some success.

In addition, her photos were attractive. She was tall - thankfully I was six foot one. What I found appealing, also, was that she had short hair.

I sent her a wink, waited a few hours and then sent her an email.

Even though one sends out these messages with great hope, it is always a surprise to me when anyone replies.

She replied within an hour.

Two days later we met for coffee and I was all prepared for a conversation about food. I had spent some evenings watching the food channel on television and I thought that she might respond positively when I told her this. I had also followed Gord's advice and taken a look at Epicurious.com.

While we enjoyed our coffee I mentioned to her something about a chicken recipe that I had seen on Epicurious.com and she said she loved chicken.

When I had clicked on the link to the site two days before, and the home page had opened, a large rectangular window popped up, with the title: *Find A Rec-*

ipe.

I could think of nothing and felt this might be a bad start.

But then, out of nowhere, a chicken recipe had appeared right in front of me. There was even a beautiful picture of the final dish.

When I told Magdalene this I could see in her eyes that she was interested. In fact we got so involved, talking about these things, that she ordered a second cup of coffee.

I thought we might just be a match.

She was so keen to get into the cooking thing that she agreed to come to my house on that Friday evening.

I said I would have everything ready.

I rushed out the next day to buy the ingredients for the recipe for Braised Chicken with Asparagus, Peas, and Melted Leeks:

- *2 medium leeks, white and light-green parts only, cut crosswise into 1/3-inch rounds*
- *1/4 cup olive oil, divided*
- *2 teaspoons kosher salt, divided*
- *1/4 teaspoon freshly ground black pepper, plus more*
- *2 teaspoons whole fennel seeds*
- *8 bone-in chicken thighs (about 4 pounds)*
- *1/2 cup dry white wine*
- *1 1/2 cups low-sodium chicken broth*
- *3/4 pound medium asparagus, trimmed, cut crosswise in half and on the bias*
- *2 cups shelled fresh peas (from about 2 pounds pods) or frozen peas, thawed*
- *1 tablespoon plus 1/2 teaspoon finely grated lemon zest,*

divided
- *2 teaspoons fresh lemon juice*
- *3 tablespoons chopped dill*

I also printed out the preparation sheet from the site. I wondered if perhaps it was a Jewish site because the recipe called for *kosher salt*. I did not know what kosher salt was so decided to take the word out of the list before I printed it.

It looked fine without the word, I thought.

I also wondered about the *melted leeks*, and tried to imagine how one melted vegetables - perhaps in the microwave - but decided the preparation sheet would explain this.

Three days later there was a knock on my door.

Magdalene was very tall.

She gave me a big smile, and a hug, although this meant getting an introduction to most of her bosom only. Even on my tiptoes I could not reach the top of her head.

Remembering that Magdalene had also mentioned a *cuddle on the couch* in her profile, I became concerned about the size of mine, but then realised that the food was more important right then.

She had brought wine, and a *Taste* magazine which she immediately opened to show me. I smiled, as though it was something I recognised.

She asked me for some wine so I opened her bottle.

I took two glasses out of the cabinet, poured more into her glass than mine, and we said cheers as we clinked them.

"So, braised chicken is it?"

I smiled, raised my index finger indicating that I had not forgotten anything, and handed her the recipe preparation sheet.

"Great!" she said. "So where is it?"

I turned her around and revealed the fresh ingredients behind us. She stared at the pile of food next to the sink on the granite counter.

Her face dropped.

Perhaps she recognised that the salt was not kosher, I thought.

"So, we're do-ing this to-ge-ther," she said.

I detected from the tone of her voice that something was wrong.

"Oh, silly me!" she added. "I thought you had already cooked the meal..."

Gord had said nothing about cooking.

I thought that buying everything for them was *itself* the treat.

And then I recalled a comment Gord had made many months before when we had first encountered each another. He had done the guessing thing I usually subjected Canadians to when they asked where I came from originally. For some reason most people start with New Zealand. I shake my head, they then go from Australia to England, and eventually come around to South Africa.

"Canadian women love the South African accent." Gord had said. "You shouldn't have any problem dating here."

Right there in my kitchen was a Canadian woman that was having a problem with me.

I didn't know where to look. It had not occurred to me, even once, that I should have done the cooking also.

"Never mind," she said taking another long sip of wine. "We can do this."

It was my first real cooking experience, and although I was very nervous we managed to get the dish prepared. Magdalene showed me how to *melt* leeks and I thought that this might be the start of something new in my life.

I decided that in the future I would consult Merle over Skype should I wish to cook anything again.

I told Magdalene about Merle, and she said she thought this was a good idea.

All the way during the meal I found myself eyeing Magdalene on the chair, and then my couch. I knew that soon we would find out whether it was large enough.

And then it was as if she read my mind.

"I do have some rules," said Magdalene as she helped herself to some more delicious chicken and leeks, and another sip of wine. "No kissing on the first date."

She looked at me. I smiled and nodded.

Of course, no kissing.

"Only on the second, if things go well, or maybe the third."

I nodded again.

The she added: "And then not a French kiss for the first one, either."

I was beginning to worry that I might forget something. Her rules were even more complicated than the recipe.

I began to wonder if perhaps we could leave one or more of the rules out, just as I had left out the Kosher salt.

"No touching below the panty line until the fourth date."

I began to uncurl the fingers on my left hand that was on my lap, to remember the list.

And as if she was timing the delivery of the final rule, she waited for me to take another mouthful, and said: "And no penetration until at least the seventh date."

My last piece of half-chewed chicken and melted leek came flying out, through my nose. I excused myself and went to recover in the washroom.

On the way back I thought it might be best to write all this down while it was fresh in my mind, but when I returned Magdalene was already clearing the table.

We did end up on the couch which was just large enough, and after putting some music on, we chatted about food. And then she left.

I thought it best not to say anything to Gord, unless he specifically asked, because I was embarrassed about the chicken coming out of my nose. And also he didn't strike me as a man who could cook, so talking about the ingredients or the recipe might not have been of interest to him. I wondered if his son cooked.

Magdalene emailed me the following week.

By this time I had already skyped Merle.

"Ja, man. Die beste is 'n lekker kerrie." *The best is a nice curry.*

She convinced me that it was easy and talked me

through it.

"You can always add some *lekker* chillies. I know you like chillies," she said.

Merle knew me well.

I liked chillies.

Magdalene was enthralled with my announcement that I would do the cooking the next time. I thought I detected excitement in her voice; perhaps even enough for her to maybe do away with one or two of the rules.

The recipe Merle gave me was with mutton which was not easy to find. After four attempts I found some, frozen from New Zealand, in the South African shop in Langely.

Her recipe also required some apricots and apricot jam - this was typical of a Cape Malay curry. The Western Cape is famous for its dried fruit.

I had always wondered what that delicious sweet taste in the curries were. Now I knew.

I bought the ingredients, laid them all out on the counter and read the recipe instructions three times, very carefully. I could at least follow instructions.

Luckily for me, Magdalene had been very specific about the fact that she loved spicy food.

I had also made sure that I bought two bottles of Packo Curried Chillies from the South African shop. They were a special chilli grown and bottled in Durban which was known for their Indian curries.

Although this was a Cape Malay dish, the chillies would be fine, said Merle.

I opened the jar. The chillies were packed in tightly and the aroma reminded me of many dishes back in

Cape Town and I had a few tears running down my cheeks when I had finished chopping them up. Whether this was from the memory of Cape Town, or the chillies I was not sure.

Perhaps a bit of both.

I mixed them in with the onion and garlic.

And I decided that I would pull out four whole curried chillies from the jar, and put them to one side, covered, for garnish, when Magdalene came.

Magdalene was so excited she wanted to come over that weekend, but I resisted. I felt that because I had not ever cooked such an exotic meal, I would do it for myself first to see how it all came out.

It was delicious.

Putting in the yoghurt and apricot jam just before serving did the trick. And the curried chillies, crunched whole right at the end, made me think that I was really getting the hang of things.

I decided that when she came, I would have a jar of yoghurt just in case her mouth burned too much.

Yoghurt was always a good idea.

And bananas. With lemon squeezed over them. To cool the mouth down.

I emailed Magdalene that same night and told her I was ready. She replied immediately, as she was online at the time.

We set a date for the following Friday evening.

I was nervous.

"Maar jy het mos die kerrie gekook, né?" But you have already cooked the curry, eh? said Merle on skype on the following Thursday.

I said I had. But I was still nervous.

"*Doen net wat die resep sê,*" said Merle. Just do what the recipe says.

I decided to cook it that evening, the day before. Merle said that a curry was always better the day afterwards.

"Just don't put in the apricot jam or the yoghurt - leave that for tomorrow, nê?"

I said I would.

I slept well that night, feeling that I had done due diligence, as the Canadians say, and that my preparations would result in a pleasant evening.

Magdalene arrived, early.

This time with two bottles of wine, and two magazines.

"I found you some recipes for curry from various parts of the world," she said in a very buoyant mood.

I had the curry simmering on the stove.

"Oh, my god. That smells so good!"

We sat for a while at the counter while she paged through the magazines.

I had some music playing and Magdalene decided she wanted to dance. I was not one for quenching anyone's enthusiasm so I danced with her.

I had put on a collection of songs from the Cape Malay Group which included *Spoek* (ghost), *Diekie Boy* and *Alibama*.

It was difficult to return to our seats with such music and we danced so much we almost forgot to eat.

Magdalene collapsed on the couch, giggling. I was sure it was also the wine and not just the music, so I was determined to serve dinner as soon as possible.

There is one dish I had always been able to make

well, and that is rice. The only rice I used was Tastic from South Africa.

I told Magdalene how ironic it was that Tastic, from Cape Town, used to ship raw rice over from America, process and repack it, and then ship it all the way back to the South African shop in Canada.

She had never eaten yellow rice before.

We sat down, but only after I had changed the music to something more romantic.

Soft Eros Ramazzotti ballads.

The curry tasted even better than my experimental one the previous week.

I was pleased with myself.

Magdalene said that it was not as spicy as she had imagined. I would have used the word *hot*, but in Canada people don't know what I mean. They say spicy.

I said not to worry. I had something I had saved for the end.

Magdalene poured us each another glass of wine. I noticed that she put more into her glass than mine. But I didn't mind.

I produced the curried chillies, and also the small jar of yoghurt and the plate of bananas which had already been on the table for us to enjoy.

"Oh, are these what you had in the curry?"

I told her that I was one of the few that could actually chew one whole. She leaned across the table, and smiled at me. "So you think you're hot, do you?"

She giggled loudly.

I felt the evening was going well.

In order to show the way, I crunched one of the chillies. The heat burst into my mouth against my tongue and I drew my breath in.

Magdalene did the same.

"Oh, man. Wow! That's some heat, eh?!" She breathed in and out and then added, "that's great. I can feel myself floating here. It gets the endorphins all churned up inside my head!"

I knew what she meant, finishing the first one. Chillies did that to me also - put me into a very relaxed state.

Magdalene picked the second one up in her fingers and rubbed the chilly down its side.

"This oil is delicious. Hot! But really good. I can see why you put it in the curry."

She split open the chilli with her thumb nail and popped the seeds out.

"I think I'll do that again, but perhaps without the seeds this time, if you don't mind."

She carefully took each one out and put them on her plate.

I was impressed with her daring. I had never before been able to entice anyone to try one of the chillies, raw.

When she had finished, I brought her a paper napkin and she wiped her hands dry.

We finished the wine and sat for a while, quiet, listening to Eros.

"Let's go sit on the couch," said Magdalene.

It struck me then that she had not yet mentioned any one of her rules. Perhaps my cooking, the curry and the Cape Malay music had accelerated me further forward.

Perhaps she might even consider this the third

date. Or the fourth, with a French kiss.

We sank down into the couch, exhausted with the culinary success.

I closed my eyes, feeling relaxed.

Magdalene moved closer to me and began nibbling at my ear.

I wondered what it was with that ear.

She then began to unbutton my shirt.

I felt I dare not move. And mindful of her rules, I did not try to touch her in any way.

She was stroking my stomach, her fingers reaching further down, below my belt.

I was unprepared for what then happened.

The dopamine had begun seeping through my brain, and I was feeling very content. What with being calmed by this chemical that relieved the stress of the chilli's heat, the wine, the curry and the music, I was floating.

I didn't think that I would be able to move even had I wanted to.

But before I knew it Magdalene had loosened my belt and slipped her fingers down to that soft unmentionable place.

When her fingers reached their final goal I felt as though instead of drinking white wine I had rather taken in some jet fuel.

My butt took off like a rocket and I felt a great cry come from deep within me.

The chillies embedded on her fingers were the fire that got me going.

I had all but forgotten what rule number we were onto just then, but I knew that if I didn't find something cool, quickly, I might lose a part of my body that I considered precious. Suddenly I knew what *melted* really meant.

By this time we were both up off the couch.

I was dancing around, not sure whether to pacify my dangling and less than majestic looking member with my own hands, or whether that would make things worse.

"Oh, my god! It's the chilly!" said Magdalene. "Here, put on some yoghurt!"

She picked up the jar and smeared it all over my diminished member. But not even the yoghurt could get the burning to subside.

I felt I was on fire.

"Come to the washroom! Quickly!"

I ran down the passage after her, my pants around my ankles, and offered my precious member to the flowing water in the hand basin.

I was in such pain, and felt my left eye going squint. I was terrified I might end up looking like the *Little Alien* just before he fell over onto his side.

It took a few minutes before I could breathe regularly and I discovered, there and then, the secret to life - *breathe in, breathe out*.

It now became the most satisfying thing I had ever done.

I wondered whether this was what Magdalene had meant when she had said: *"So you think you're hot, do you?"*

It occurred to me that perhaps this was her way of making sure that her date-rule number seven remained in force for a long time. And when I thought about that number seven I realised that I had no intention of using my member to penetrate anything even vaguely warm, never mind hot.

I can say no more about this episode, except that for many months I did not touch that jar of curried chillies I put back in the fridge.

But whenever I did open the fridge and my eyes wondered over to the shelf in the door where I kept those curried chillies, I had a very funny sensation down below, and my groin grew quite tight with fright.

I am sure it was The Universe reminding me that there are far worse things than just being squint, and secretly I apologised to the *Little Man* for any insult I might have caused him when making fun of his squint eye.

And his tongue.

8

Serving Papers

I said nothing to Gord about the abuse of my family jewels when I saw him again. I could sense that he was in a bad mood, anyway, as he did not enquire about my latest escapade.

Besides, I didn't think he knew anything about curried chillies. After all, people in Canada don't even talk about hot food. They call it spicy, as I have already said.

I sat in the sauna next to him, thinking that I might have been happier to deal with spicy rather than with the heat I had endured.

I decided also, after consultation with Merle, that I would take a short break from trying to impress women with recipes.

She did say that I should keep cooking, just in case. I did.

In fact I became an expert cooking Bobotie - *bub-*

boe-tee.

This is one of the signature dishes of South Africa.

Particularly the Cape Province.

To be quite accurate, as Merle often reminds me, most everything that is good comes from the Cape which is also known as The Cape of Storms - the name given to this location by the Portuguese.

Not only the food that arrived with the Malaysian slaves, but also the wine that arrived with the Huguenots from France have made this province famous all over the world.

Merle is sensitive enough to remind me that when I say things like this - that there is no need to leave the Cape, as it has the best of everything - it is an insult to people who live in the old Transvaal.

Or the Transkei, for instance.

Or KwaZulu Natal.

I said that I had no particular feelings on the subject but that I was simply repeating what she often told me and also what I remember Uncle Storky had always said. I think it was one of the few things that he and Oom Athol always agreed on, and they would often raise their glasses to celebrate this.

Not necessarily that all good things came from the Cape, but that they both agreed on something.

I am grateful that the Portuguese arrived at the Cape. I was reminded of their talent with food when I found myself in Canada, and encountered a Nando's Chicken franchise.

Don't get me wrong - they didn't perfect chicken only. I once heard a tourist say, at the Victoria and Alfred Waterfront in Cape Town, that nobody can cook fish like the Portuguese.

I think they are right.

They also have their own spicy gift to food: it is called peri-peri. It was Weimaraner Diaz who alerted me to the benefits of peri-peri when I was young. He had always said that there was something special about this Portuguese sauce.

One day I asked Oom Athol about Weimaraner's name, and he told me the whole story.

Apparently, in the sixties, a Herr Hans August from Weimar, about 80 kilometres southwest of Leipzig Germany had bought a farm on the outskirts of Stellenbosch, and had employed Vernon Diaz as a farm worker.

Vernon apparently won Herr August over when he managed to produce a bunch of dead rabbits each Friday. Herr August was particularly impressed, because he loved eating rabbits, but could also not understand why, when he had specially-bred Weimaraners from Germany - dogs that were bred to catch rabbits - they never came home with any.

Herr August spoke so highly of Vernon Diaz to his other employees, telling them that they should follow his example, that the farm community started calling Vernon *Weimaraner*.

Each week, on a Friday afternoon, Weimaraner presented at least three freshly killed rabbits to Herr August.

Oom Athol said it was a mystery to the German farmer, because his dogs never came home with any rabbits. No matter how hard he worked them on his farm.

Not only did Weimaraner manage this, but he also introduced Herr August to peri-peri. Of course he never told him that it came from the Portuguese. He told him that his wife had invented it, and made it in her kitchen.

According to Oom Athol, Herr August went wild when he tasted it. Especially when he used it to marinade the rabbit before slow cooking it.

In fact, according to Oom Athol who was distant family of Weimaraner Diaz, Herr August paid Weimaraner a fortune for the recipe and tried to patent the sauce, by using the African Bird's Eye Chilli discovered by the Portuguese in the first place.

He even called it *peri-peri*.

Unfortunately things did not turn out well for Weimaraner when Herr August found out that the Portuguese had been using peri-peri for years, all over the world.

Things went from bad to worse when he had a visit from a farmer who had a large farm up against the Hottentots Holland Mountain range.

Especially when it turned out that this farmer bred rabbits.

I had recovered from my sabbatical and took a peek at Match.com again.

I had four winks and three favourites, and two matches. The one was a women with a large car, so I deleted her.

The other was of Portuguese origin. I immediately thought of cooking something with peri-peri for her, but then remembered that I had stopped using food to impress women.

She was a lawyer.

I consulted Gord.

"Does she have any dogs?" he asked.

I said that I had twice scanned her pictures - there had been four: two outside some court. One at home on a deck looking at the sunset. And one in Mexico.

"The dog could be lurking somewhere," he warned. "Ask her straight out."

I said I would.

We began communicating via the site. She was busy the following week, but agreed to a meeting the week thereafter. I did ask about dogs and she said she was a cat person.

Her name was Andréa.

I prepared myself for the meeting.

I tried to think of as many Portuguese stories as I could, but all that came to mind was Weimaraner and Herr August.

And Weimaraner's divorce.

I was beginning to wonder whether my resolve to stop trying to impress women with my food was such a good idea. After all, I was sure that Epicurious.com or even Jamie Oliver would probably have a recipe with peri-peri.

Perhaps even one with rabbit.

But then I remembered the jar of chillies sitting in the door of the fridge back home, and decided against it.

The meeting went well enough. I thought it best to focus on her entirely and not tell her about the Portuguese in South Africa. Or bother to mention peri-peri.

I asked her about her work; she said she spent a few days of her week in court. Mostly with divorce cases.

She asked about my work. I told her that I was retired.

"So you have an adequate pension."

I smiled, and nodded.

"So is it just a pension, or is it adequate?"

I told her it was both.

It was her time to nod.

"More coffee for you?"

I told her that I had only one cup a day, and that was decaf. She asked if I was allergic to caffeine. I said that I just felt it was not good for me.

"So doesn't decaf coffee still have some caffeine in it?" she asked.

I said not really; perhaps just a *residual* amount.

"Oh. So what's the difference between *some* and *a residual amount*? she asked.

I smiled as though I didn't really understand and decided it was time I focussed on something else so asked, straight out, whether she owned a Bel Air.

She looked a little peeved, even though she smiled.

"No, I have a Lexus."

I smiled and nodded, feeling relieved.

I must admit I had been feeling I was under some scrutiny, as if in court. But I did like the sound of her voice, and she looked very professional.

I could not imagine her roaring down Marine Drive in a V8.

I began to wonder whether she had any date-rules. I considered asking her straight out before a date, but decided against it. I don't think she was used to having anyone asking her questions. It was probably always the other way around in court.

We sat is silence, and then I got to thinking of Weimaraner's divorce.

It was a sad affair.

In fact after the sale of the recipe and the visit from the rabbit farmer over the hill, Weimaraner's fortunes turned for the worst.

He began drinking heavily again and soon Oom Athol was talking about him and his wife getting divorced, in the pub.

I had spent two years in the army, fighting the Cubans on the Border in Angola, and then came home. Unluckily for me I had been classified as a white by the apartheid government. Had I been coloured, like Emma I would not have been called up to fight.

My father had asked me what I wanted to do. I had vaguely mentioned law. Frankly the idea of debating issues quietly in a courtroom, after various military encounters in the bush, seemed to appeal to me.

In truth, I had no idea what I wanted to do.

He arranged for me to spend a week in court, and it so happened that Oom Athol and his wife arrived one day to show support for Weimaraner's wife at the final divorce hearing.

In South Africa, this is always in the supreme court, and not a magistrate's court.

I was sitting near the front because my father had made me go in early each morning. Although as a citizen I did not need permission to enter, my father had singled out this particular court because the judge was a friend of his.

Mrs Diaz sat demurely to one side.

I could see that divorce proceedings were not pleasant. I had spent the previous two days witnessing this.

It is like a death, and very sad.

And to make matters worse, it cannot be easy to stand up in court and speak of one's troubles. Especially when one needs to remember a long list of questions asked by one's advocate.

I had gotten used to the procedure. But it was easy, sitting down in the gallery. It was another thing standing, and talking about the failure of one's marriage, while responding to questions from one's lawyer.

And then having to remember to look the judge in the eye when delivering the answer. And *not* the advocate.

Even I got confused every now and then. And I wasn't even the one asking for a divorce.

Mrs Diaz seemed flustered when it was her turn.

"Please state your name for the court," said the advocate - the first of many routine questions.

She did.

He went on to ask her about their children.

Then about the marriage itself, which meant asking about her husband.

This was the confusing part, because every now and then she would refer to him as *Weimaraner*, and the stenographer would raise her left eyebrow, the judge would raise his right, and the advocate would raise his fist to his mouth, and cough.

She would then have to correct herself and give his proper legal name.

"State his full name for the court, please," said the advocate quickly.

She did.

"And his date of birth."

She did.

Thereafter the advocate must have gotten the sequence wrong, because he suddenly jumped to another matter.

Instead of asking the routine question *how long has he resided in South Africa*, to which Mrs Diaz had been prepped for the proper answer, he said:

"You said also, Mrs Diaz, that he is an alcoholic."

She replied that he was.

"How long has he been an alcoholic?" he asked, looking at her with his head cocked to one side.

"Since birth, Your Honour," she said, looking at the judge.

Some people in the court burst out laughing.

This time the judge coughed.

I felt so sorry for Mrs Diaz standing there all alone in that dock and having to face these strangers.

But then she seemed to be relieved also as she began to giggle.

They eventually established that he had lived in South Africa since birth, and had been an alcoholic since working for Herr August.

When I began to tell the story to Andréa, she seemed less interested in Mrs Diaz, which I felt was strange as Mrs Diaz shared the same name as the Portuguese explorer - Bartholomew Diaz - who had been the first person to round the Cape of Good Hope.

She seemed far more interested in the court procedure in South Africa where attorneys and advocates perform different roles.

I told her as much as I could, but then when she began asking technical questions I felt a little like Mrs Diaz in court that day and began to falter with some of the answers.

I decided we should change the subject. So I asked her if she would like to meet again.

"Oh, yes, that would be fine," Andréa said, taking another sip of coffee, "when?"

I said any time that would please her.

Apparently she did have dating rules, and came out with one immediately.

"I just want you to know that if we do get on, and see one another again, I will want to take a look at your papers."

Once again it felt like a court appearance, and I suddenly thought of Magdalene and the couch, and wondered whether my prospects with her might not be better.

Somehow I could not imagine Andréa coming anywhere near my couch.

I had seen nothing in her profile about cuddling.

I began to strike all these possibilities off the list - *Portuguese cooking*, *cuddling*, the *couch* and then there was the fact that I wasn't even *divorced*.

Perhaps, as a divorce lawyer, she dated only divorced men to gather experience. I tried to think whether I had selected the wrong radio-button somewhere on the site, and had chosen the divorced option.

I didn't want to ask her whether she dated divorced men only, but then I couldn't imagine that she was wanting me to produce the burial papers of my late wife, in lieu of a divorce decree.

Eventually after some silence I plucked up the courage and told her that I wasn't divorced.

"Oh, not the divorce papers. Test results," she said.

I was just being silly, I said smiling, although I had no idea what she meant.

We left it at that and instead of inviting her to my empty couch and a counter full of ingredients, I suggested a walk the following Saturday.

She agreed, saying she would check her schedule and email me before Wednesday.

She did.

We met up that Saturday evening, around six at False Creek. It was a beautiful sunny day and after a long walk, with her pointing out various apartments across the water, saying she knew the owners and how much they had settled for, we sat down for a drink at a small local pub on the water.

I felt we were going nowhere with the dating-rule she had presented, which in fact had sounded more like an ultimatum.

I dived straight in, and asked her, with a smile, so that I could change it into a joke, where I could get such papers from.

"Oh, the papers? Well, any hospital; there are also lab clinics all over the place. But phone your doctor first, otherwise you will have to pay."

I sipped my beer slowly, thinking that perhaps I

should have splashed out and bought an Innis & Gunn with 7% alcohol, rather than the Honey Brown I had on the table with only 5% in it.

Another two percent might have jolted some memory deep inside.

I tried to think hard, as I focussed on a yachtsman, single-handedly, trying to tie up his small sloop to a buoy in the water below us.

Lab. Hospital. Papers.

I took another sip.

I had been thinking of legal papers.

Andréa got busy texting on her phone, after she apologised to me.

I sat with my beer and continued to watch the yachtsman. He had missed the buoy and his yacht was now slowly moving on a collision course with another tethered boat.

For some reason I recalled my other court visit.

After the divorce Oom Athol had felt sorry for Weimaraner, and when he lost his job on the farm, he had employed him as a driver.

I think Oom Athol had simply assumed that Weimaraner had enough experience.

When he and Oom Athol came the following week, not to the supreme court but this time to the magistrate's court in Wynberg, there was clear evidence that he had not anything of the kind.

My father had said I had seen enough divorces, and he was worried I would get used to them. He felt I should get a taste of real life in the local magistrate's court.

He knew the magistrate - Blackie Swart. They were

old friends from the time we had lived in Simon's Town.

It was rather strange, but it would be the second time I saw Oom Athol in court. This time Uncle Storky came with him for support.

Apparently Weimaraner had been in Oom Athol's bakkie (pick-up truck) on a delivery.

"Can you explain to us," said the prosecutor, "exactly where you were, and what you were doing."

"Yes, your Onna (Honour). I was in the bakkie."

We waited.

"Yes, but why? And what were you doing?"

"I was trying to get pass this man in his car, but his car stopped dead, right there in the street. He said there was something wrong with his alternator."

"With the alternator of his car?"

Weimaraner stared at him.

Having had to grapple with the difference between *some* decaf and the *residual amount* I knew now how he must have felt back then.

The prosecutor seemed unflustered, and repeated what he had said, as though this kind of confusion took place every day. Which, of course, it did.

"Yes, Mr Diaz, but you were on your way somewhere. We need to establish your line of work and the nature of your business on that particular day."

It must have been the long sentence because Weimaraner looked very vague.

Oom Athol began to grow impatient.

"Man, sê net vir hom waarheen jy oppad was!" he shouted in desperation. Man, just tell him where you were going!

Weimaraner said he was going to drop something off at Mrs Lavender.

"Let's move on. You stated that the complainant, Mr De Venter, was in a stationary car in the middle of the road. And that you could not get passed him."

Clearly Weimaraner was unable to process more than one statement or question - the alcohol had clearly taken its toll over the years.

He stared at Oom Athol.

"Ja, man!" shouted Oom Athol.

"Silence!" said Blackie Swart. "Only witnesses being questioned may speak in my courtroom please."

"Yes, Your Honour," said Oom Athol.

Uncle Storky pocked him with his elbow.

"Ja," said Weimaraner, "he was blocking me. I couldn't puss him."

"Can you please explain to us what happened next?" asked the prosecutor.

Weimaraner looked keen to tell his story. In fact he almost climbed over the dock railing.

"Mr De Venter got out of his car."

We waited. And waited. Clearly Weimaraner was waiting for affirmation.

The judge coughed.

He started up again.

"And he comes over to me and he says, 'man, can you do me a favour, my alternator has pecked up and my battery is flet.' "

"When you say *his* battery, you mean the battery of his car?" said the prosecutor.

Weimaraner looked very confused.

"My fok, ja!" shouted Oom Athol. For f#$k-sake,

yes!

"If there are any more outbursts, I will clear the gallery," said Blackie Swart, the magistrate.

"Ja!" shouted Weimaraner.

The prosecutor continued: "Now, let me get this straight, Mr De Venter came over to you and told you the battery of his car was flet. Sorry, I mean flat?"

"Yes. I already said thet," said Weimaraner, getting cocky.

"And what else did he usk you, sorry I mean *ask* you to do?" said the prosecutor, suddenly looking flustered.

"Ja," said Weimaraner thinking again, "he asked me to poes him."

There was silence in the court. One could hear a pin drop. The women all looked down, and only one or two men smiled. But very demurely.

The word he had uttered was particularly crude in Afrikaans, and it referred to the most critical genital part of the female species.

He might not have chosen a dirtier word, even though it was only as a result of the inflection itself.

Of course he had meant *push*.

I was waiting for the prosecutor to ask for elaboration, but he didn't.

"He asked you to poe-push him?"

Weimaraner looked confused, as though the people around him were crazy, asking the same questions over and over. And arguing about whose alternator it was.

Now, remembering the story, I could only sympathise with this poor man - to have every word one says scrutinised, and dissected.

"Ja, so I poesed him," he said finally.

"Nog nooit!" shouted Mr De Venter from one corner, *No ways!*

"Quiet please," said Blackie Swart. "You will get your turn."

"Hy't my gevra om sy kar te poes!" He asked me to push his car, Weimaraner said quickly, just to make sure.

There was silence.

After a while Blackie Swart said, "Can we perhaps not just move forward a little. Mr De Venter can *you* please tell us what happened."

"Yes, Your Honour. I asked Mr Diaz if he could give my car a nudge."

"And what did he say?" asked the prosecutor before the magistrate could get another word in.

"He said it was fine. I mean he had a rubber bumper, and so did I. I told him that I would have to put the car into second gear, and that it was called a push-start. Of course I was hoping the nudge would get me moving, and then I would be able to let the clutch out to start the car."

Weimaraner nodded in agreement: *"Ja, dis wat hy gesê het!"* That's what he told me.

"Mr Diaz. What did you then do?" asked the prosecutor, determined to stick to protocol with his witness.

"Your hon-nah. I just toll you. I did what he said. I reverse the car. I start the bakkie in first gear. Then second. Then I poes him."

The penny didn't drop for a while, except it was no

news to Oom Athol whose *bakkie* - truck - was severely damaged.

Or to Mr De Venter.

"So, Mr De Venter. Carry on," said the magistrate.

"Well, Mr Diaz reversed. I was sitting in the driver's seat waiting for the nudge, ready to let the clutch out. I thought he had buggered off. Sorry, Your Honour, I mean driven off. I looked in my rear view mirror again, hoping to see Mr Diaz's car up against the back of mine. Instead he had reversed down the road and was coming towards me at high speed."

"Jy't gesê (you told me) second gear!" shouted Weimaraner.

This was too much for Oom Athol.

"Jou stew-pitt idioot! Hy't gevra vir 'n nudge. Nie 'n fokken collision nie!" You stupid idiot; he asked for a nudge, not a f#%cking collision!

He jumped right over the railings of the gallery for spectators, and began to throttle poor old Weimaraner right there in front of the magistrate.

The court case ended in chaos, with the magistrate ordering everyone outside.

Oom Athol went to jail for four days.

Weimaraner got a warning, and Uncle Storky spent the four days Oom Athol was in jail, telling the story to anyone who would listen in the bar, saying over and over that this is what comes from someone who was afraid to go up North during the war.

I was now worried about these papers. I started to feel that some things had been a little easier in the war I had fought in the bush, all those years ago.

I could not imagine that there might be anything amiss with my Canadian citizenship papers.

But then I remembered she had spoken about the hospital. Perhaps it was the medical we had had in South Africa before we arrived that she was talking about.

I thought of poor old Oom Athol in jail. And I wondered whether remembering the story of Weimaraner and Oom Athol was perhaps the Universe warning me about something.

Even though the jails in Canada take all possible human rights into account, and have televisions and carpets, I wasn't sure that any nookie was worth a sojourn there.

I started to panic.

She finished texting.

"So," she said," it's been lovely. I'd like to see you again. But without the papers we can only be friends."

I smiled broadly, but felt I was none the wiser.

"No, it's not a federal medical," said Gord the next day. "Or emigration."

I waited for it. Something worse?

"She wants you to be tested."

Tested? DNA?

I wondered if I should ask Gord whether perhaps she felt I was black because I came from Africa.

As always, he seemed to be able to read my thoughts.

"Like for STD's and stuff. Like she's saying she won't go to bed with you without you being clear."

I sat back against the wooden bench. I had heard

of animals being tested for genetic lineage, or dogs for rabies. But never potential dates for a clean bill of health.

I sighed.

The last time I had given blood I had passed out, quicker than Blikkies when he walked into Maria's wedding uninvited, but that's another story.

I wondered whether it might be better if I phoned Sharon to find out how Sparky was doing.

Or even the Little Alien.

I went for the test.

Luckily for me there is a Tim Horton's coffee shop in the hospital.

I didn't pass out, but I had to buy a coffee and two doughnuts before I could walk out of the front door, and across the car park back to my car.

I sat there savouring one with honey dipping, wondering how I had fallen from grace.

After a short culinary career, here I was minus most of my blood, eating processed doughnuts.

I presented the papers to Andréa. She looked down at the results with her glasses perched on the edge of her nose.

"HIV?"

I looked dead ahead.

"HIV is also part of the whole thing; I wonder why they didn't test you for that," said Andréa putting the paper(s) down.

Right there, sitting with Andréa on the deck at Hemmingways, in White Rock, and looking out across the bay with the sun's heavy afternoon rays starting to dance in the water, I felt ashamed that I almost wished for Sharon to come down in her Bel Air.

Had she done so, I might have jumped over the railings myself, just like Oom Athol in the court that day, and right into the back of Sharon's car. I imagined myself turning around, and waving to Andréa as we grumbled down the strip away from her.

Instead I summoned the waitron and ordered another pint of Innis & Gunn, with rum finish. This was a slightly different taste, with them maturing the beer in barrels of rum, rather than barrels of whisky.

Darker, and more ominous.

I felt I needed something more complex to contemplate the way forward.

I wondered whether *any* nookie was worth bleeding all over the place. Again.

I sighed.

"I am sorry," said Andréa, looking almost gracious. "But we don't know each other, do we? I mean, you could have been anywhere, in any country. It is the same for me. I am separated, but haven't been with anyone since my husband."

I smiled dutifully. Yes, Your Honour, I thought.

The waitron returned with my beer. I took a sip and was on the verge of asking whether she had received papers from her husband on a regular basis, but then I thought better of it.

I returned to the clinic the next week, after spending some hours on *pof* and match.com. Sadly I found few, if any good looking women without large dogs, small dogs, or cars.

I bled again.

Now I had two sets of papers and far less blood inside of me.

Andréa disappeared.

Apparently the separation with her husband was not going well.

We did speak on the phone a few weeks later.

She said she was delighted that I had thought enough of her. Of *us*.

And that she was hoping that in addition to the HIV, I had also remembered to get a result for hepatitis.

I said nothing.

I thought of poor old Mr De Venter sitting in his car back then, and waiting for a nudge.

For some reason I felt strongly that any more negotiations with Andréa and I would end up, not on the couch with any kind of nudge, but probably with some form of collision damage.

Perhaps with me coming off even worse than Oom Athol's bakkie that day.

After serious thought, I decided to go back to cooking as a means to find someone and leave Andréa to her own legal devices.

After all I had my bobotie recipe under my belt in more ways than one. I just needed to find a woman who loved food; again.

I told Gord I was finished with lawyers. He said nothing.

I think in his mind he was far busier with his move to Kelowna.

When Merle heard about my resolve, she was delighted.

"Jus leave the chillies out this time. Stick with the

bobotie. It's simple, man. They will love it..."

I agreed.

And when I tell this story, of my brush with the law, to some of my friends both in Cape Town and even in Canada, I always tell them what happened to Weimaraner because I feel it is the right thing to do.

I had to return to that same magistrate court in Wynberg, where Blackie Swart had been the magistrate. And where Oom Athol had been convicted for disrupting the proceedings, and where he had been sent to jail.

Some years later my father had had the need for the delivery of some important legal papers to the magistrate's office and he had asked me to take them.

Inside the entrance of the building I ran into Weimaraner.

He had sobered up entirely.

He now held the position of Assistant to The Messenger Of The Court, who was known to the locals as *Hasie Hendriks* - Rabbit Hendriks. I had heard Oom Athol talking about him.

One of Weimaraner's primary functions was to serve papers on members of the public required to appear before the magistrate.

He walked with me to Blackie Swart's office that day, and when I had delivered the papers, he took me to his own little office.

He was so proud of the fact that he had one.

It was a tiny space, perhaps just the size of a large closet.

I noticed in the corner against the wall, there hung

a rabbit.

"Hasie Hendriks loves rabbits!" he said, winking at me.

After all those confusing questions Weimaraner had to endure in the courtroom that day, and his own brush with the law, he had finally found his place in the world.

And now thinking of that story I wondered whether, in my bid to find a companion and my new resolve to go back to cooking, I would ever find mine again.

9

LA PETITE MORT

When I saw Gord again there seemed to be a change that had come over him.

Like a visitation. He became quite animated.

Apparently he had a doctor friend who had announced to him that all or most of the bad cholesterol was to be found in carbohydrates.

And not in fat.

Looking down at his stomach, Gord said he had perhaps finally found a way to lose weight.

Not that I am in any way an expert on stomachs, but I did mention to him that if one stood relaxed up against a wall and then allowed one's head to drop down, one should be able to see one's toes.

Gord obviously tried this at home because a few days later he announced that his toes were short.

In deference to his size and sensibilities, I had not taken this any further.

"It's all about sugar," he said looking at me, this time. Gord very seldom, if ever, looked at me. I felt something was brewing.

"And that means carbs. So it's no good avoiding just processed sugar. The carbs are full of them too."

He looked at me again.

I felt very much under the limelight and looked down at my stomach quickly. It was decidedly smaller than his but nevertheless, there in the sauna, in full view.

I knew that although I swam in the pool daily, ate as healthily as I could, there was no doubt that my stomach clearly indicated that I was somewhat partial to beer.

And I knew that beer had lots of carbs.

As if reading my mind, which Gord always managed to do, he said: "And it's no good giving up pasta and potatoes, and then drinking beer..." I felt that there was a little snigger at the end of this announcement.

My heart sank.

Clearly I loved beer, but if there is one type of beer I do not like, it is pale ale, and especially the Indian Pale Ale. To my mind, one is either a sweet person, or a bitter person. Or the type of person who drinks any kind of beer.

I cannot drink just any kind of beer.

It should not be bitter otherwise I find myself wondering why I started drinking in the first place. And I don't want to do that because I once read a quote by someone who said that he got more out of alcohol than alcohol got out of him.

I am sure it was Churchill, and because my father

revered Jannie Smuts, and General Smuts and Churchill were friends and confidants, I usually take both of them at their word.

So I do not want to start debating about whether to drink or not.

I simply settle for being the kind of beer drinker that does not like a bitter aftertaste.

Even visiting my cousin in England reminds me of this fact.

When I am there visiting, my favourite thing is to go out with her husband and have a pint at the local pub. Because I like beer.

I also like her husband very much which of course helps things immensely.

I grew up with an idea of British pubs: old buildings oozing with character, black wooden beams and long, solid wooden counters with beer pump handles sticking out, like fingers beckoning one to come closer.

South Africa as I said before had very few pubs in the previous era - we had what we called bars, but men were not allowed to have a drink in them with any woman.

Not even if they were white.

And we, Emma and I, had further difficulties, as I have said, because she was not classified as white and that meant we sometimes got into some trouble.

When my cousin's husband laughs at this - not at the fact that Emma and I were not the same colour - but at the fact that we could not go into any bar together even if we were, I feel a little silly because of course the law was very silly.

The only way we could drink with our womenfolk

was go to a hotel that had a ladies bar.

When he shakes his head at me, I remind him that it was still punishable with a jail sentence to be gay in England until 1967. I was twelve back then.

And I remind him that the world was a strange place in those days even though two years later a man walked on the Moon.

And because her husband and I seldom dwell on sexuality - him being British - and I am embarrassed about the apartheid era, we usually quickly change the subject.

And most often we get to talking about beer.

I sometimes share with him my opinion that even though the English copied the European monks and developed their own beer industry, I do think they were too busy still drinking mead, because to my mind they were not paying attention.

The beer there, in England, is warm. And flat. Imagine drinking a warm beer, with no bubbles, I ask myself. Of course it is no use asking him, because he doesn't know the difference.

The sad thing is that the British think that I am the strange one when I point this out.

I make sure he always takes me to a pub that has at least Newcastle or Guinness on tap, because the rest of their beer? Well, there is something wrong with it.

I mention this to him every time, but when he gives me a funny look, like when I talk about ladies bars, I just say the world is a funny place and only some people know how to make proper beer. And then we agree that he is entitled to his opinion, and I to mine.

And we sometimes even revert to talking about

sex because beer to an Englishman is often more important. And perhaps it is not a good idea to remind him that their beer is dull.

Now I am sure you are wondering how it is that I can drink Guinness when I don't like bitter beer.

Well, even though I get some strange looks from the bartender, I ask him or her very nicely to splash a little lemonade or Sprite into the bottom of the glass before pouring in the Guinness.

And that takes care of that.

And if anyone looks at me funny, I remind them that there is a famous cocktail called *Purple Guinness* with blackcurrant. And another called *Black Velvet* with Guinness and champagne.

And then I remind my cousin's husband that I had to come all the way from Africa to tell people in England that it is okay to squirt a little lemonade in the bottom of a Guinness glass. And this is especially surprising considering that we didn't even have pubs in South Africa until around 1991, as I have said.

As you know I now live in Canada. And I do think that although South Africa has the third largest brewery in the world, with a long history, Canada is right when it says, *we (Canada) did not invent beer, we just perfected it.*

I was sceptical at first when my Emma and I emigrated there, as you can imagine. Especially after my visits to Great Britain, and the fact that Emma and I emigrated to *British* Columbia.

I was expecting the worst.

But when I tasted the Canadian draught beers, I realised they definitely knew what they were doing.

None of this warm stuff, I was grateful to discover - like they don't have fridges in England?

I know that you might be thinking that in Canada because it is so cold we don't need fridges. But that is not true - the insides of buildings are very warm. And thank goodness Canadians know how to cool their beer before pouring it.

And so it was, when moving to Canada, I fell in love with their beer.

And I didn't have to embarrass myself by asking the bartender to pour some cool drink - pop - into the bottom of the Guinness glass. I discovered that they have a wide range of wonderful draughts that settle very nicely in my stomach - and of course that is the problem.

All except the pale ales.

They are just too bitter for my liking, and I could never understand why people would want to come to the end of their day after many trials and difficulties, and then settle down with a bitter taste in their mouths in order to relax.

And so sitting there with Gord and realising that I preferred sweeter beer to anything with a bitter after-taste, I realised I was in trouble because in all likelihood sweeter beer had even more carbs.

My heart sank.

Perhaps Gord felt that eating too many carbs was linked to finding a good date. Perhaps he was simply on a mission to improve his own health. I wasn't entirely sure, but he did not let the issue go.

"I have stopped eating bread," he announced one day quite loudly, and in front of two men we didn't know and who were sitting on either side of him.

It amazed me how often we conducted our dating strategies in the presence of strangers.

I told him that I had stopped eating bread years before when Emma had come home one day and had told me that my flatulence, and what she called brain fog, was because I was allergic to yeast.

I had stopped and both had disappeared.

Gord seemed satisfied, but I detected that his nose might be a little out of joint at hearing that I had made some progress without having to take his advice because he quickly added, "Yes, but what about pasta, rice, cakes and puddings?"

I told him I never had puddings at the end of a meal. And I had cut down on pasta also.

But sadly I was addicted to rice. I did not think I could live without rice. I said nothing about this, but nodded when it came to the pasta, and just to cover myself, I mumbled the word *pasta* when I did so. But left out the word rice so as not to incriminate myself entirely.

"Cakes are the problem," said Gord quite loudly again.

I asked him why, in particular.

"My girlfriend bakes amazing cakes. And I used to have a slice each day. Now I have to stop."

Gord's enthusiastic announcements petered out and I got the idea that he had gone into some kind of mourning at the loss of his daily slice of cake.

He didn't seem to want to continue the discussion and we both fell silent, and it brought the discussion about food to a halt for quite some time.

As fate would have it two days later I got a message from a Judy.

She said she had messaged me some months before without response. I could not remember any communication from her and immediately felt guilty that I had perhaps had too many meetings.

I stared at her picture. She was petite. Short hair. A big smile. I shook my head because I could not remember her at all. I even checked my favourites that were stored on my profile, but she was not there.

She wanted to know if I wanted to meet.

I checked her profile for small dogs; large dogs. For vintage or muscle-cars. Any legal reference, pictures of trains and any reference to chillies or *spicy* food.

None.

I said yes.

Because I was getting a little tired of False Creek - if anyone can get tired of such a beautiful setting - and of the ubiquitous pub and beer, I was delighted when she mentioned a French restaurant on the water in White Rock itself. It had a genuine French chef.

I was surprised Judy suggested meeting at four in the afternoon, and wondered what she had in mind to eat.

I soon found out.

"I just love their cake," she said.

I shook my head, smiling.

"Why? Don't you like cake? You don't have to have any, if you don't want."

I raised my hand indicating that there was no problem.

"Oh, he's wonderful. The chef, I mean. Trained in

France. His dishes are amaaazing," said Judy with a broad smile. "I come here as often as I can."

And then she leant forward as if she needed to whisper.

"I'm hoping he might apprentice me, you know. Maybe I even get to visit France, and learn to cook."

She flicked her eyebrows up and down which I felt looked a bit strange.

It seemed that food was very much a part of her life. I considered mentioning my bobotie. But then I thought of the carbs Gord had spoken about, and after I noticed the stern expression of the French chef behind the counter while he cooked, I decided I would keep any suggestions about food to myself.

"Would you like to order yourself?"

The intonation of Judy's voice sounded like a gentle prompting to allow her to make the suggestion and lead the way.

Keeping in mind that I could cook only bobotie, I told her as demurely as I could that I knew nothing about French pastries.

She impressed me even more when she ordered something in French.

While we waited we chatted about food, and her dream of going to France to learn to cook.

I tried to be as diplomatic as I could, and said I was sure it would be just a finishing-school experience for her, as I was in no doubt that she was already fantastic in the kitchen.

She giggled, and then sat back in her seat staring at me with a big smile of her face.

I felt the bit about being good in the kitchen might

have come out wrong. And I wondered what she was thinking.

The cakes arrived immediately after our tea.

I had ordered Earl Grey, with sugar. It was the only tea I drank with processed sugar and even though I sometimes felt guilty about it, what with Gord's warning about sugar fresh in my mind, I made a mental note to have a smaller portion of pasta that evening to compensate.

"It's called a Paris-Brest," said Judy confidently and looking at me.

Of course she did not spell the name out to me, so my mind might have done some somersaults on hearing the pronunciation, had I been so inclined. But I simply nodded without smiling, as I felt a smile might give something away.

I was grateful it looked nothing like a breast at all.

It was certainly round, but where any nipple might have been there was a hole which made it look far more like a doughnut.

The fresh choux pastry was almost steaming, and peaked out from underneath flaky hazelnuts that were covered in icing sugar dust.

There was not much that announced it from an aesthetic point of view, but the reputation of the French as cooks clearly became centre stage when we took a bite.

Because I was wary of showing that I knew anything about cooking, and had decided I would keep all my recipes to myself, I needed to rely on Judy's reaction to give some indication as to the outcome of this gastronomic episode. And so held back myself.

She closed her eyes, squirmed slowly but effortlessly in her seat, and seemed to be transported to quite another place.

It was a place that I imagined people might want to go to - this, just because of the expression on her face.

And I wondered whether I had, perhaps, made the journey myself because there was something familiar there in that expression: as she allowed the pastry and the cream to travel between her palette and her tongue, she opened her mouth as if to confirm the source of her ecstasy. I could see why she wanted to spend time in France.

And right there I was reminded of a saying the French have: la petite mort - the little death.

I think the loss of consciousness the French talk about when using this expression is clear indication that when true ecstasy arrives, it sometimes means that one has to give something up, and allow it to die so that a true transformation, a resurrection might take place.

Clearly Judy found herself here, in this cake. And it seemed to lure her towards a destiny she seemed unable to resist.

I made sure that I smiled broadly when I took a bite myself, but held back on closing my eyes and squirming in my seat.

What with thoughts of breasts and little deaths forefront in my mind, I didn't want to give her the impression that I was an expert on such matters. Gastronomic, or otherwise. Especially on the first date.

Unfortunately for me what happened next, Judy decided to show that she was indeed an expert.

"It's positively orgasmic, don't you think?!"

I had just taken a sip of tea and, before I could swallow, my body's reaction was quite unlike her own.

I sneezed the entire mouthful of tea through my nose.

It burned.

And then, of course, I began to cough and in order to cool my nose down, desperately sucked the remaining tea and cool air back inside.

"Oh, my! Didn't you like it?"

For no reason I could think of I felt the need to recover the brown tea that was now spread across the white table cloth, and so began to wipe it with my napkin in my embarrassment.

It was some time before I could speak, but when I could I told Judy that it was amazing.

And while I did not wish to focus entirely on the cake itself or French cooking because, as I have indicated, I did not want to give any impression that I knew anything about food in case Judy decided to test my ability to cook, I did decide to find some way of paying her a compliment. Perhaps to make amends for my terrible display.

I remember Merle once saying to me in her off the cuff street-wisdom manner: *"Jy moet nooit vir 'n meisie sê sy's vet nie!"* You should never tell a girl she is fat.

I would have thought that was obvious.

But then years later, I remembered reading in a magazine that one should never even mention to a woman that she was slender, or thin. In fact, this article went on to say that one should not focus on size at all, but simply say that she was looking healthy or fit.

I mentioned this to her. I tried hard not to have the true thoughts in my mind when I said this - that I was surprised to see how thin she was, what with all her cake eating.

"Oh, I am just lucky. I must have a very fast metabolism, because I never put on weight."

Clearly I was the kind of person that allowed my thoughts to be read, loudly.

I was about to tell her about Gord's new revelation with regard to carbs and sugar but immediately realised it was a very bad idea.

We finished our French-Brests and tea, and went for a walk in the afternoon sunshine.

It was July, and hot enough to make us seek out some shade on the promenade.

I got to thinking that sometimes a cake like the one we had treated ourselves to can also be a gift. Despite the carbs, and the sugar.

It was there, sitting on a small bench together that I was reminded of Mr Solomon in Simon's Town, back in South Africa so many years before.

Judy could clearly see that some deep memory was surfacing, and she graciously asked me what it was.

I told her we had moved to Simon's Town when my father was called back to the naval base for a series of court-martials. He and my mother decided to settle in a navy house overlooking False Bay and the many ships below.

I must have been in primary school, probably around grade five.

It was long before I met Emma.

We found ourselves in the old Royal Navy laundry offices, now converted into a house. It was, then, the highest house in Simon's Town, right under the cableway that used to ferry supplies from the base itself below to the sanatorium high up above us, on top of the mountain.

In fact, I seem to remember my mother saying that patients were also transported to and from the naval hospital just below us.

I was soon to learn that Simon's Town and some other pockets of Cape Town were somewhat special in that the apartheid government did not always apply the segregation laws as strictly as they did in other locations.

At least immediately.

We had a number of streets populated by Muslim people who, strictly speaking, were classified as non-white.

In fact Mr Manuel, the tailor, was the preferred stop for all naval officers when promoted and new ribbons had to be added to their uniforms. A mosque took pride of place down below us, near the main road and the entrance to the base itself.

As a young man I knew two things when walking down the main road of Simon's Town: one was that this small town somehow contained the most beautiful looking girls I had ever seen. And two, my innate understanding, even as a young boy, was that they would be unavailable to me because I was white.

When I fell in love with my Emma years later, I always wondered what happened to me down there, on the main road of Simon's Town, and the awakening that might have taken place, looking at the beautiful Muslim girls walking down the street in front of me, with their jet black hair cascading down their slender backs as though it were some kind of exotic waterfall.

Because when I first saw her, my Emma, she reminded me of them. And at first, I was afraid that I had fallen in love with her because she simply represented something that was forbidden to me.

But after spending so many years with her, I realised that this was not true, and that I had loved her because she had been given to me as a gift.

I remember thinking that Mr Solomon had also been something of a gift.

My mother had discovered him.

At the bottom of our driveway, that turned very sharply to the right in order to go down, through the Royal Naval hospital buildings that were now occupied by the Naval Band, was a high corrugated iron fence.

One day, while planting flowers in a large pot my mother had beckoned me to stop talking and to listen.

"There's someone on the other side of the fence. Can you hear that singing?"

I said that I could hear something, but was not sure what it was.

"Hello?!" My mother could never resist a challenge.

"Good afternoon, Ma'am."

"It's a beautiful afternoon, isn't it?" my mother asked.

She told the voice her name. "What is your name?"

A somewhat diminished voice came through the iron fence, and with my face stuck as close as I could get without burning my skin on the hot surface, I thought I could see a small shack-like structure in the distance, and the presence of a body close to my eye.

"My name is Mr Solomon, Ma'am. Thank you ..."

"We heard your singing. I didn't know there was anybody living there."

There was silence.

My mother waited without response, and then eventually continued with her gardening.

That night at the dinner table my mother said something that shocked me. It was my coming of age in a sense, in the era of segregation and forced removals that managed to mould and manipulate all of us.

For me, it was something I still had to fully understand. But sitting there, at the dinner table, I was acutely aware that a moment had arrived.

"I think he is coloured," she said.

I stared at her blankly. Why would she say that?

"I think, when I said that I didn't know he was living there...; I think he perhaps thought I might report him, or something."

My father said nothing. I could see a look on his face that expressed both concern and irritation.

My father had been an owner-builder of many houses, and I had grown up with coloured gentleman artisans and technicians all around me, on the building sites. They came to our house in Bergvliet to collect money and to report to my father. And my mother always served them tea and cake.

To me they were part of my life and our social structure.

It came as a rude awakening that my mother had singled Mr Solomon out in this way.

Something of a little death, but quite unlike that Judy might have experienced.

During the following week I noticed my mother down at the fence a number of times. I knew she was listening to make sure he was still there.

That Saturday, she baked, as always, her weekend cake. But this time she baked a second one, smaller. Enough for one person. One man, perhaps.

And then I saw her walking down the driveway to the fence with that cake in her hands.

There, she called Mr Solomon.

I moved closer so I could see and hear what might happen next.

"Hello Ma'am," said a voice from the other side.

I could see my mother relaxing.

"Mr Solomon, I baked a cake for us and thought you might also like some. I hope you don't mind and that your wife might not be offended?"

She lifted the yellow plate above her head and over the fence.

An old hand reached out and took the plate.

"Oh, no Ma'am. My wife passed on years ago. I am living alone. This is beautiful. Thank you."

I could see that my mother was now satisfied. They were friends.

From that day on my mother baked Mr Solomon a cake every Saturday.

Something told me that this was a highlight for him, and the delight in his voice each time was some indication of this.

He would return the yellow plate the following Saturday, quite clean and in a little brown paper bag, over the fence, and swap it for a new yellow plate and another cake.

Without ever seeing one another, they would exchange words about the weather, and the beautiful view of the bay below that we all enjoyed, and then Mr Solomon would disappear for another week.

One day my father came home looking miserable.

"I think Mr Solomon's days are numbered," he said.

Sadly, even at this young age, I knew what he meant.

The following Saturday, I told my mother I was going to take the cake to him myself.

She smiled and handed the yellow plate to me.

I walked down the hill, following the fence to the bottom of the road, and then looked up to my left. There, up against a bushy outcrop sat Mr Solomon outside his small house.

I managed to cross the large drain in front of me, and walked, with difficultly, up the barren hillside that was mostly clay and with just a few eager weeds forcing themselves out of the ground.

"Good afternoon, Mr Solomon," I said.

"Good afternoon. So you live over the fence?"

"Yes," I said.

Mr Solomon got up and went inside his little house. He came out with a small chair, put it down on the ground and sat on it.

I stared at the chair he had been using. It was more sophisticated, with armrests and a torn plastic cushion back. I was just a young boy, and here was a grown man giving me his chair.

It was difficult for me, and I did not know what to do.

"Come sit down," he said to me. And he took the yellow plate inside, and then came out with two small slices of cake, one each on a plate of its own. The plate he used, I noticed, had a chip on the edge.

"I look forward, each Saturday, to your mother's cake. She is a very good cook."

It was just as well that we did not know anything about carbs, and sugar in those days. We simply enjoyed every treat we were given.

I smiled, feeling somehow at the same time at home, and also very uncomfortable, there next to him.

And then after a long silence, he said: "Can you please give your mother something?"

I nodded.

He went inside, and came out with the yellow plate, empty and clean. And a small piece of paper.

It was folded. I stared at it in my fingers. There underneath and upside down, was the shaky writing of someone that might have been either very old or very young.

I put it in my pocket, and we continued to sit in silence, enjoying the morning sun and the view of the boats that looked so small in the bay beneath us.

I asked him where his wife was. He told me she was buried behind the house up against the mountainside.

He looked sad.

Here was an old, gnarled coloured man and a white

child, together. I remember that is what I felt that day, and I knew that it was unusual.

But we were together, and there I felt a oneness that made me want to stay with him.

On his side of the fence.

And something told me that it was an important moment - like one of those one can never repeat. Or one that signals the end of something and the beginning of something else.

Eventually he said to me, as though he had sensed something, and ending. "I think you will be fine. You will meet someone very special one day. I know..."

It was the kind of pronouncement someone might make after much time of consultation, or negotiation, or advice. It felt a little strange.

And he pointed his finger to his head, as though the picture was there inside. And I wondered what he could see.

I got up and said goodbye, and walked home with the plate and the little note to give to my mother.

Two weeks later my father came home and said Mr Solomon would have nowhere to stay because he had to move out of his little house. I stared at him.

At dinner that night he announced he would invite him stay in the room at the bottom of the old laundry building.

A few days later I woke up to singing.

My father smiled.

"He is singing church songs. Not exactly my cup of tea," my father said laughing.

But things changed that night.

It seems that in the morning Mr Solomon greeted

God, and in the evening he celebrated Life because he sang the Blues and many jazz numbers my father was familiar with, but that were new to me.

I used to creep down the side of the building before supper each day, fearful of him seeing me, and stand up against the wall listening to his singing.

It was sad and lonely, and uplifting at the same time.

I never knew what Mr Solomon did, or where he went during the day. But each evening he was back in his little room, singing.

This went on for about two months.

And each Saturday, my mother walked around the building, called to Mr Solomon and gave him a small cake. And I used to be behind my mother, and would hope he would invite me inside to sit with him.

He always did.

But one day I suggested we go back to the house and sit there, so we would have the view. Mr Solomon looked very sad, and he shook his head and said, "I think it is better that we sit together here, and share the cake."

And so we did. We shared he cake, and many things - things of the heart.

But then one day the songs stopped.

My father cocked his head that morning at breakfast. He didn't say anything, but I knew he was listening for Mr Solomon.

I crept around the building and stood at the door of his room. I raised my hand to knock, but then ran away.

Two days later my father entered the room to find

it empty.

He came home that night to say that nobody knew where Mr Solomon was.

For some reason he looked at me. It was not a look of incrimination. It was a look of inquiry. As though he felt I might know something.

I shrugged my shoulders.

But then when I joined him outside after dinner, and sat next to him while he smoked his pipe I felt a heaviness in my heart, because I sensed I might know where he was.

My father looked at me and said nothing.

We got up together. He held my hand as we walked down the driveway towards the old iron fence, then down the road, around the bottom where the fence came to an end, and then up the mountainside to the little house now abandoned.

I stood at the side of the house and pointed to the tree behind, at the back.

My father nodded, and walked up there alone.

When he came down, he smiled at me and gave me a hug.

"You were right," he said.

When we got home, he took my mother in his arms.

"He's next to his wife's grave, lying on the ground. Tomorrow I will have to make arrangements for someone to fetch and bury him. Perhaps there next to her. But probably not."

There was no doubt in my mind that this was the end of an era in our lives. And in particular, mine.

So much more than just the songs had stopped.

Everything seemed to change. The next term my mother sent me to boarding school.

The day we left home she made me cupcakes. She packed them neatly into a tuck box for me. I was in my brand new uniform, all dressed up and feeling very frightened.

There were three cupcakes left over that would not fit into the tuck box.

I ate two of them.

And then I took the last one and walked up to Mr Solomon's house.

There I saw his wife's grave for the first time. But Mr Solomon was not lying next to her where he had wanted to be. They had taken him, far away from her.

I knelt down and put the last cupcake on the ground next to her, where my father said he had laid down and died.

I began to walk down the hill, but then turned and looked up again. And I noticed that the cupcake's icing was yellow.

I smiled.

And even though I hated boarding school so much and was bullied so often, I always remembered that iconic moment, sitting on that hill with my Mr Solomon, overlooking the bay and the boats.

And I remembered his prophesy of hope: that I would find someone special one day.

And it always kept me going.

Because that day the singing stopped when I went to boarding school. That day was just like a *la petite mort* - very much unlike the loss of consciousness in a moment of ecstasy that the French mean when they use this term, and much unlike the one Judy might have experienced when eating her Paris-Brest in that French restaurant that day.

But a real death.

I had lost my innocence and found the harsh, cruel reality of Life.

And it was only when Emma came into my life that I truly started living again.

And in many ways those songs in my own heart had a chance to be revived when we met.

And with her, I could sometimes hear them. In the morning, and some evenings. And even though she is now gone, I still hear them if I listen carefully.

And so it is that when I eat a cake, especially if it is a Paris-Brest, I cannot help but think of Mr Solomon, and the joy my mother's cakes had brought him.

And those precious moments we had shared.

And the death I felt with his passing, and my having to go to boarding school when I was so little.

10

The Right Ingredient

After my mishap with Magdalene, I decided I now understood what a woman expected when she came to my home for a meal.

I was also feeling more confident about my much-improved cooking skills, and felt if my mother had been able to bring Mr Solomon so much joy with hers, I might be able to do the same for someone special.

With this in mind, and more lab results than the average patient in a hospital bed, I decided to start looking for a woman without dogs, cars or a legal profession.

And one who also liked to eat.

Preferably not just Paris-Brests, though.

This time I wasn't going to discriminate in any way, and would look for all body types and not, as before, only those who were average or had a few extra pounds.

After all, it would be the eating that would be the hook, and I wasn't going to allow any prejudice on my part to interfere with this.

In fact, while I was busy searching over the period of a week or so, Merle even taught me to make *melktert* - milk tart.

This was a particularly famous South African speciality that involves cooking milk. When Merle first told me I said no, because I didn't like the idea of boiling milk. I hated the taste of caramel.

"It's not caramel, Oom! Jus listen to me and do what I say!"

Merle got a little upset so I listened to her, followed the recipe and tried my best to make her proud.

"It's going to work this time," said Merle, "trust me. Everyone loves my melktert. When I gave the recipe to Dikbek De Villiers' wife he couldn't stop smiling for a week, man!"

Merle thought this was very funny and laughed merrily when we skyped that day.

She gave me the ingredients.

"Just follow the recipe. If the first one doesn't come out *lekker*, we skype again to see what's wrong."

I thought it was a good plan. I typed out the ingredients carefully:

- *400 g (14 ounces) puff pastry or flaky pastry (see tips, below)*
- *500 ml (2 cups) full-cream milk (whole milk)*
- *1 stick cinnamon*
- *3 eggs, separated*

- *80 ml (1/3 cup) cake flour*
- *15 ml (1 tablespoon) cornflour (cornstarch)*
- *80 ml (1/3 cup) castor sugar (superfine sugar — regular sugar may be substituted)*
- *2 ml (1/2 teaspoon) baking powder*
- *30 g (30 ml) (2 tablespoons) butter*
- *15 ml (1 tablespoon) vanilla essence (vanilla extract)*
- *ground cinnamon*

In fact I got so excited about this new project, and my new-found vision that I could entice a woman with my culinary skills, I doubled up and cooked two melkterts.

They did not taste that good.

I consulted Merle. She made me take all the containers and cartons out of the garbage.

She was not impressed when I realised that I had used soy milk instead of full cream dairy milk.

I told Merle it was not my fault because there are so many different types of milks in supermarket fridges in Canada, that even an experienced cook like myself could get confused.

I tried again.

This time I cooked only one.

I was sorry I did, because when that melktert finally cooled down and I scooped up a slice, I thought it was better than even Merle's melktert.

But, of course, I told Merle the next Saturday morning on skype that it was *almost* as tasty as hers.

"Jislaaik! You getting good, né?!"

I told her she had to come out to White Rock, to see America just across the bay, and eat my melktert.

"Nee, man. Kry vir jou 'n egte tert!" *No, man. Get*

yourself a real tart!" she said with a chuckle.

We laughed at the joke, and I realised how much I missed Cape Town and its people, and felt so privileged I still had family there. Merle was family.

I decided I would go out there, and make her bobotie and a melktert one day.

That Sunday I changed my profile, taking out anything to do with *intellectual stimulation* and replaced it with a more confident paragraph on how much I loved cooking.

I was sure that the bobotie and the melktert would do it.

Finally.

I felt that all I had gone through was in preparation for this moment. The more I ate that melktert, and the more I scanned Match.com, the more confident I felt.

I was getting so good, I felt confident I could smell danger from a long way off. Just like Blikkies Adonis could detect the sweet-smelling perfume coming down the road, from far off, or like Uncle Storky when he just knew Oom Athol was talking *kak*.

I was confident I had developed a nose for detecting the profiles I should avoid, and those I should investigate. Just like I could detect from those first two melkterts that something was wrong.

I skipped through a long list of names and faces that I felt I knew, instinctively, were not for me. They were either too professional, or there was a dog lurking in the background, or sitting on their laps.

If I read anything about skiing, snowboarding, kayaking, dogs, cars or intellectual stimulation, I probed no further.

I was exhausted after two hours, but then suddenly I felt I might have found someone.

Her screen-name was *cuddlesforcooking*.

I was not entirely sure whether she wanted the cuddle if I cooked, or whether I was to give her cuddles if *she* cooked.

But then I thought maybe if she had said it the other way around - *cookingforcuddles*, she probably meant that *she* would cook and then I would have to give *her* a cuddle. My head was spinning, like a top.

I took a deep breath and thought about it with a cup of Rooibos tea.

I decided that her username meant that she expected *me* to cook.

I decided to find out.

We emailed a few times, and then I sent her my phone number. She phoned at an appointed time.

Her name was Jennifer.

"A man who can cook!?" She seemed the happy sort, and did not in any way sound sarcastic about this.

I told her I had two special recipes.

I was careful not to mention anything about chillies.

We decided to have the obligatory meeting.

We met for coffee. It went very well.

She was average height, a brunette with a big smile. There was one thing that got me - when she smiled her eyes went very narrow, and small. It was always something I found attractive. In fact, I thought she was very pretty. And as a bonus she also had short hair which made her even more so to me.

I didn't tell her that immediately, but kept it in the back of my mind. For just before the first cuddle.

She was not a lawyer.

I told her a little about Sparky and the Bel Air, without too many details. Of course, I said nothing about what Sparky did to my leg. Or the legs of that poor policewoman.

"Oh, no. I have two cats. But they never travel. So when I go out, I am all alone." She smiled.

She asked me what I loved to cook and I told her a little about the bobotie - that it was a Cape Malay dish with very mild, but tasty spices. She seemed intrigued, and we agreed that she would come to my home the following Friday evening, and I would cook for her.

She was a teacher; of French, and Social Studies.

She told me that the social studies included Geography.

I imagined that I would impress her with a little geographical knowledge of my own - my cooking from The Cape Of Storms in South Africa, and also some wine from the surrounding region.

I mentioned that Cape Town had the oldest vineyards in the world outside of France. And that the Western Cape province was one of only six floral kingdoms in the world. I also told her that the oldest mountain in the world, Table Mountain, had more species of flowers than all of England, Scotland, Wales, and Ireland put together. I was certain this would impress her.

Suddenly she started sneezing. She quickly reached into her purse and covered her face with a tissue. Whatever there was up her nose seemed to want to come out very badly.

"Oh, just some pollen in the air," she said, eventually. "It's that time of the year. I am sensitive to pollen. And also to gluten. Is there any gluten in the Bobotie?"

She sneezed again.

I tried to picture the list of ingredients.

I could not remember any gluten. I said I didn't think there was any.

I was worried that all the talk of flowers in the Western Cape had set her off like that.

"Yeah. I have to take a pill if I eat a dish that has gluten," she added. And then she said, "Thank goodness I haven't passed this sensitivity onto my granddaughter."

She looked at me. I quickly showed interest by smiling and raising my eyebrows slightly.

She fumbled in her purse, again, for her phone, selected the album and flicked through to show me Chevon - a pretty two-year old girl.

Chevon had a bush of red hair, and looked a little like Judy Garland in The Wizard of Oz. I wondered what the mother and father looked like.

I told her it was a lovely picture. She chatted about Chevon for some time, but I didn't mind. I had a way with small children and I told her I would like to meet her.

It was a good strategy, saying nice things to a grandmother about her grandchildren, I thought.

I could not wait to see what my bobotie and melktert did.

Soon afterwards, she had to leave for an appointment. I walked her to her car, and when she drove off she opened her window, stuck her arm out and waved at me.

It was a very good sign, I thought. And it made me feel special. I felt strongly, right there, that this could be a match.

But I could not get the image of that red-haired child out of my mind.

My father's brother always told a great story of one of his patients, years ago. Uncle James had been a gynaecologist of some note in Cape Town.

It was on his desk that I remember seeing, as a child, the plaque that would one day be very common, and which read: *so many women, such little time.*

When Uncle James had had more than one glass of wine he would tell stories of women, and babies, because those were the only ones he knew.

There had been this one emergency case of a single mother, who came off the street. She had not known she was pregnant. Uncle James said that this was sometimes possible, in rare cases, even right till the end. She had gone into a public toilet and her waters had broken.

The ambulance brought her into the hospital and Uncle James had been on duty that night.

Very soon a baby boy popped out. He had done so with a crop of red hair 'erupting like flames from his head,' as Uncle James always said.

Uncle James handed the child to the mother to feed and asked her, out of curiosity because she had very dark hair, what the father's hair looked like.

"*Haai, Dokter. Hoe moet ek nou wiet? Hy't 'n keppie opgehad!*" Doctor, how should I know? He had a hood on, she had said.

Her surname was Mavis Khilla.

Of course, when having dinner, and Uncle James told this story it always brought the house down.

But then he always saved the best for last.

"Believe it or not," Uncle James always said, taking a sip of wine at just the right moment, "Mavis named that poor child Cyreal!"

Thankfully he told this story many times over because it was years of growing up before I realised why this was so funny.

"So you're going for the cooking angle again?" asked Gord in the sauna the next day.

I said I was.

I also said that I had stayed clear of chillies this time. But I did mention Jennifer was sensitive or allergic to gluten.

"That could be a problem. What does she look like?" he asked, wiping the sweat from his brow.

I told him she was really cute.

"So, no dogs, no cars?"

I said not.

"Bikes?"

I said after speaking to her I didn't think so.

He nodded.

"You do know that a woman with a car, like that one with the dog? That's pretty rare?"

I said I hoped so.

"There are probably more out there with bikes. Have you come across any?" he asked, looking at me.

"No," I said.

"That could be fun."

I tried to think why. And I promised myself that if I did have to resort to a lady with a bike, I would not sit behind her.

"Sometimes they have more than one," said Gord, reading my mind again.

I didn't know why he was on about bikes, especially when I had been so enthusiastic about a new culinary venture. I told him I was going to stick to Bobotie and Melktert.

The next day, I got nervous about the ingredients and phoned Jennifer. I said that I had definitely checked, and there was no gluten in the Bobotie.

Or the blatjang - pronounced, *blutt-young*.

She wanted to know what this was, and I told her that it was chutney. It was impossible to eat Bobotie without chutney.

I had always thought this was the Afrikaans word for chutney, but one day at Kuala Lumpur airport, I realised that it was a Malaysian word.

The Malaysian immigrants had introduced many new words to the Cape. And there were many European words we had given to them, also.

Some of Merle's family had many names of Greek Gods or Roman soldiers. For instance, one of her uncles was Titus November. Merle told me that many slave owners had named their favourite pets after their heroes in history. When the slaves were set free, and they had to register their names with the magistrate, most of them simply adopted the names of these pets.

No doubt because the slave owners had treated

them so well - the pets, not necessarily the slaves.

I told Jennifer about the word blatjang itself, where it came from and soon we were talking about some of the Roman names the original slaves had adopted.

She seemed fascinated and commented that it was probably not unlike some men today. She told me about a date she had enjoyed with a man whose screen-name had been Dikkus Maximus. She asked if I knew which Roman hero this was. I said I was not entirely sure, but might do some research.

I didn't want to alarm her in any way, but felt that she was more qualified to tell me why he had chosen that name.

Thankfully, she did not mention him again.

Jennifer said she wasn't sure about the chutney, and would probably have to check the ingredients, as they sometimes put soy sauce in condiments, and soy sauce had gluten.

I said that it was definitely a sauce cooked with mostly fruits and spices. And that if the spices for the Bobotie were fine with her, she wouldn't have any issues with the blatjang.

I was sure that was that. But there was a short silence on the other end of the phone.

"I can't eat certain fruits, especially if they're picked from a tree."

I said nothing.

"It's the pollen," she said.

I said that I could not imagine there would be any pollen in the fruit as it was boiled, and cooked for hours when making blatjang.

She said that she might try just a little, as cooked fruit was okay.

I found a pen when we had finished talking, and a yellow sticky note, and wrote down: gluten, fruits picked from trees.

I stuck the note to my computer screen, so that when I was searching for recipes, or talking to Merle it would be available.

That following week I went over the Bobotie recipe again and again. I searched in vain for gluten. And even asked Merle if blatjang had any fruit picked from trees, and with pollen on.

"She sounds like she's *vol fiemies*," she said quickly. I said she was worth a try, even though at times she appeared fussy.

I cooked both the Bobotie and the melktert on the Thursday. Both would taste better when Jennifer came that Friday evening.

She arrived, as Canadians do, spot on time: 6:30.

She brought no Taste magazine or wine. Instead she brought some Belgian chocolates. I thought they might go well on the couch later with the cuddle I was looking forward to.

We sat outside on my deck, looking down at Semiahmoo Bay and some yachts on the water. It was a beautiful Spring day in White Rock, and we marvelled at the fact that even though it was only late April, the temperature was above 22 °C.

I thought it might be a good strategy, while we waited for the Bobotie to warm up, to ask about Chevon. I was sometimes bad with names, so I had written her name down on the sticky-pad, with the warning about gluten and fruit picked from trees.

"Oh, she's a delight," said Jennifer. If we became friends, would you like to meet her?"

I said I would like that very much. Things were going well.

I thought about telling her the story that Uncle James had always told, but then decided that it sounded better in Afrikaans and, besides, she might think I was saying something funny about how her granddaughter was born. I didn't want her to have any bad impression about my attitude towards children, or families. Or red hair.

I asked about the parents.

"She's my daughter's child. Here, let me show you and picture of the family."

She consulted her iPhone again and flipped through an album.

I noticed that her daughter had the same blond hair as she did, but that father was the one with the red hair, probably just like the father of Cyreal Khilla.

Jennifer laughed. "Yeah, he's from Ireland. Hair as red as a burnt sunset!"

I smiled.

"They're a real mixture. What with my daughter being Anglican, and Aidan being a devout Catholic. But they are very happy together."

I poured her another glass of the Meerlust chardonnay I had bought in the local liquor store. I told her she would be enjoying the Cape that evening, what with the chardonnay and the Bobotie and melktert.

"I can't wait," she said, smiling.

The wine was sinking in well, and I felt that very little could go wrong. Jennifer was relaxed. There was no V8 parked outside, no dogs in sight, and I had not taken one peek at the jar of curried chillies since the last episode.

I had it in mind to perhaps show her one of my lab results just in case she was too shy to ask for my papers, but then decided against it.

I asked how it was that she could drink wine if she was allergic to some fruit.

She began to explain the complexities of her allergies, but after a few sentences I felt lost - what with some fruit freshly picked from a tree that was bad for her, and others she could eat without any problem. Like mangoes - she said she loved mangoes. I wondered if they grew special ones underground, but didn't' want to ask.

When she stopped to take another sip of the wine, I decided to rather tell her a story about eating. Before I became even more confused.

"Oh, I'd love to hear it - what, what's it about?"

I said that it even involved a Catholic family, so she might be able to understand.

She leant over towards me and I began.

I told her that next door to us in Simon's Town, when I was a little boy, there lived a boy called Damon. Damon was a very shy boy, and hardly ever said anything. Apparently his mother said that when he did say something for the first time in grade four, his teacher had fainted as she had never heard his voice.

One of the reasons his mother often invited me over was because he felt comfortable talking to me.

But he would do this only when not in the presence of adults - it was strange.

His mother always served him his main meal at lunch. Sometimes I would also be invited. This was a treat for me, because it meant I got to eat two big meals in one day - at lunch and also one at dinner.

Damon's mother was a devout Anglican, also, and made us both say grace before we ate each meal.

One day we were invited across the road for a play date. That family were devout Catholics. But they did things differently. They always had their main meal, just like us, at night.

We sat at the table and bowed our heads to say grace, before the mother served us. She brought in a plate of hotdogs which we devoured quickly.

When we had finished our hotdogs and drinks, the mother asked us to bow our heads again.

Both Damon and I looked around at the others. Their heads were all bowed.

They said grace again.

When I opened my eyes, I could see that Damon was looking confused.

Believe it or not, having said nothing all week, he came out with it suddenly:

"In our house we say grace only once, and we get better food than this."

I didn't know whether to laugh, or bow my head quickly just in case. Luckily the mother of our friend burst out laughing and with Damon still looking confused, she could not wait to pick up the phone to tell Damon's mother what he had said.

Jennifer found this very funny.

What with a signature Cape Malay dish, some of the best oak-matured chardonnay in the world and a funny story, I felt the evening was unfolding perfectly.

I excused myself and went inside to check on the Bobotie.

Jennifer followed me.

"Oh, I see you've even gone to the trouble of setting a beautiful table."

I did what Merle had told me, and stuck a clean knife into the middle of the Bobotie, took it out and licked it. It was perfectly warm and tasted just right.

I took the lid off the yellow rice. A small column of steam rose up to the extractor fan.

I said I was ready to dish.

I had felt the Cape music I played for Magdalene was a bad omen; I was not going to tempt fate in any way, so I had some soft jazz playing this time.

We sat down and started to eat.

"Oh, my goodness. This is good!"

Jennifer took another forkful. "It's got curry in it. But it's not too spicy. And there's something else...; what's that crunchy thing in the middle..?

I told her they were almonds. Just as I said this, I panicked. She had said nothing about nuts. I knew many people were often allergic to nuts. And could die from them. Everybody was going crazy at schools about nuts.

"Oh. I love almonds. They're even better than the cashews in Thai curry. It's amazing - Malay? Don't think I've ever had anything from Malaysia."

I swallowed my mouthful and then had a terrible thought: fruit picked from trees. The Bobotie had apple in it.

I decided to focus on another ingredient, and said I hoped that the raisins were okay, seeing as though she drank wine.

"Raisins? There are raisins in this? Oh, my god! Yes, I *can* taste them. Mmmm; sure, they're okay. I seldom eat them, but I don't have any problems with raisins."

I exhaled slowly, and took another sip of wine. The bottle was going down fast.

We were doing well. Raisins, almonds. So far, so good with the apple. I thought about mentioning the apple, but could not make up my mind. After all there was only one in the whole dish.

But then I felt guilty, so I told her there was one apple in the dish.

"In this Bobotie? Really....? I am trying to find it. Can't say that I can taste it."

I asked if it was okay.

"Oh, I'm sure it's fine, after all it's cooked, isn't it?"

I said that it was.

"No problem." She looked at me. "You *really* mustn't worry so much. As long as there's no gluten. Or milk, I'll be fine."

Milk?

I asked about the milk after taking another sip of chardonnay.

"I am allergic to the protein in all dairy. Remember I said that dairy was also a problem?"

I didn't remember.

I had gotten away with the apples, raisins, wine. But now I had to watch out for milk.

I left the table, feeling unsteady. On the way to the

kitchen I added *milk* to the sticky note on my desk.

I opened the fridge door and realised that the milk I had used was made from almonds - I had forgotten that, because the dish contained real almonds, I had asked Merle if it would be okay to use that instead of real milk.

I held both thumbs. When I got back I asked if almond milk was okay. I didn't think it was dairy.

"Oh, it's fine. That's exactly what I use all the time, especially in smoothies. I just can't have cows milk. Or cheese."

Cheese - parmesan, mozzarella? Goat's cheese?

I asked if that meant all cheese. I didn't have to wait long for an answer.

She looked despondent. "Sadly, yes. *All* cheese; even goat's cheese. But there's no cheese in this, is there?"

I said there was not.

Jennifer laughed. "Oh, it's sweet of you to be so concerned. I promise it will be *fine*."

I was beginning to feel more sorry for myself than for her. How does one cook without cheese? Or butter? Surely cooking without butter was just about impossible?

I went back to my desk and wrote down *all cheese*.

I came back to the table, sat down and exhaled deeply. I tried to remember whether I had used butter. I thought that the recipe called for either butter or vegetable oil. I was sure I had used butter. I decided I needed a short rest, and closed my eyes.

After a few seconds, I hesitatingly asked about butter.

"No problem; butter is not a problem."

I stared at her. Butter was dairy, or was I imagining it? It came from a cow, after all. I decided not to ask for any elaboration.

Besides, the sticky note was now full.

Suddenly I thought of the egg. I knew that it was often also classified as dairy.

That was the last precarious ingredient I could think of, so I faced the music, and said there were eggs in the Bobotie.

"Eggs?" said Jennifer, taking another sip of wine. "I *love* eggs! Oh, my God - omelettes? With mushrooms and tomatoes, bacon? Just no cheese."

So eggs were not dairy. That was it. I was in the clear. She had even tried the chutney and loved it.

I decided to save the melktert for the couch later.

After dinner we danced. At one point she put her head against my chest, and I lightly rubbed her back as we did a slow dance to some smooth jazz I had playing through my wireless system.

At the end of the third dance, Jennifer began to wobble. She separated herself from me, raised her hand to her forehead and walked to the couch. I followed her.

"Not feeling so good," she said.

I wondered what could possibly be the matter. We had eradicated all possible ingredients that might be bad for her.

"Something is wrong," she said. "Are you sure you used the almond milk?"

I went back to the fridge. Yes, I told her. I had used all the full cream milk for the melktert.

"Melktert?"

Suddenly it hit me. I had not known about the milk until she told me at dinner. I was grateful I had decided to save the melktert for later, which meant we would now have to avoid it.

I told her that the special tart I had baked for her had the real dairy milk.

"Oh!" she said, with her one hand rubbing her stomach.

I felt like a little boy watching his mother get sick.

"I don't feel good. Can I just lie here for a while?"

Of course, I told her. I asked if she would like a blanket.

She said yes.

I covered her with a blanket Merle had crocheted years before, and sat down on a chair and stared at her.

I wondered if I could cope with all the taboo ingredients each time we ate. I imagined there would be more ingredients that she would come out with.

The next thing it would be bread, or something.

"Are you sure there was no gluten?"

I didn't know what to say - there had been no mention of gluten anywhere.

"I do feel I have had some gluten." She rolled over, moaning some more. "Like in bread, for instance?"

I felt like I had hit a brick wall. I lowered my head into my hands. Of course there was bread in the Bobotie. That's partly what made it unique.

I confessed.

"Oh, that's not good. Bread?! Bread has gluten in it. Remember I told you?"

I did not remember.

Instead of keeping my distance on the chair, I moved and sat on the couch next to her, in the far corner, as she had taken up most of the cushion space.

I didn't know what to do.

I could hardly offer to rub her stomach - we had had only three dances, and had not even held hands yet.

But then there was no time to worry about where, or when to touch her.

Something terrible happened.

If Sparky had done damage to my new jeans that day when he jumped out of the car to greet me, it was nothing compared to the devastation the half-digested bobotie did to my freshly washed and beautifully ironed clothing when it came out of Jennifer's mouth, onto my lap.

The speed with which the contents of her stomach launched itself was greater, I am sure, than the acceleration of that Bel Air down Marine Drive on that fateful day.

And even faster than Sparky himself when launching himself in attack mode.

When she left that evening after recovering I sat alone and ate the melktert. I wondered how something so tasty could be a threat. It was comfort food, and I did feel sad that Jennifer could not share it with me.

But I decided that my career in cooking for women, whether it was for cuddles or not, was finally over.

I told her the next day that I was going away indefinitely. I think it was the first time I felt even mildly ungracious and, looking back now, I do feel a little ashamed, because I didn't phone her again.

I flew to Cape Town to take a rest, and to inform Merle of my situation. I said that I was done with dating. Even with women who were not lawyers, or ones without large dogs, small dogs or V8's. Or allergies.

That was it.

In fact I told her I was considering getting myself a dog and cooking for the two of us, rather.

However, I did feel better when I cooked Merle some Bobotie, and also a melktert.

And as we ate together, she laughed.

"Jy's baie snaaks," said Merle.

I said I didn't think any of this was funny.

But then she said something that made me think. She put the last piece of melktert into her mouth and when she had finished savouring it, she said:

"Oom, Life is sometimes like riding a horse. When you fall off, you mustn't run away. You mus' get back on that horse."

11

The Screaming Of Those Lambs

When I returned to get back on the *horse* Gord told me he had recently found someone, and they seemed as though they were having a good time and so, much of the dating conversations that took place in the sauna for a while were about his Cynthia.

"Movies," he said one day. "Find someone who loves movies - there's so much that happens when you do."

I nodded. I had no idea what had happened to the diet. I decided not to ask.

Gord grew silent, perhaps thinking of a movie he had shared that previous evening, or weekend.

"Have you seen Princess Bride?"

I said I had not.

"It's old," he said. And then he quickly added: "Make sure you don't end up with someone who likes only newer movies..."

He turned to look at me.

This was clearly something significant, for him to turn and look straight at me.

I said I would not.

"Some of the best movies are older ones...; I mean take most of Jack Nicholson's good work. Years ago."

I nodded.

"And even Titanic. Like, there's a whole generation that's never even seen it."

I had found myself thinking of Casablanca.

So it was a wake-up call to have Gord remind me that even Titanic was old.

I reminded myself, sadly, that having so many decades behind one is sometimes daunting.

"It's quite funny as well," he said.

I assumed he was still talking about Princess Bride.

"And if you can put up with the romantic ones that's a big Brownie-point, right? I mean, I really don't mind them. And it makes them happy..."

Clearly Gord had exhausted himself because he lowered his head and said nothing more.

I wondered what exactly he had meant by "...there's so much that happens when you do."

I assumed that he was talking about intellectual connections. I remembered my date with Zoe who had contacted me because of my mentioning intellectual stimulation.

I shuddered, as it had not ended well, and the picture of the Little Man's squint still haunted me.

Perhaps he had meant the other thing.

Especially because most of the movies he had mentioned were romantic in nature.

I was exhausted myself, what with the tragedy of Leila still in my mind, and my returning to Cape Town.

I felt I would be glad to escape from reality for a while.

I went home thinking that Gord had perhaps, once again, come to the rescue. And I could not help but shake my head at how something or someone up *there* seemed to be listening in to the conversations between Gord and me.

Within three days I was singled out by no fewer than four prospects. I had made their Favourites List, and with each one highlighting the fact that they especially enjoyed sharing a movie with a partner.

I ignored two, and contacted the other two with a simple text message.

Two days after that an Agnes came back to me.

I thought her profile picture was a little bland - there were only two and one was upside down. I felt it was perhaps not a good start, and wondered how she might feel if Netflix broadcast some of their movies upside down.

But out of the four original, she was the only one left.

I didn't think a meeting could do any harm.

We settled for neither a pub, nor a coffee shop nor a restaurant with fancy French pastries.

Agnes asked if we could go to a movie together. I agreed, although felt that this was a little silly, as we would probably not have much chance of getting to know each another and I felt, too, that a movie was more of a date.

But then I felt that it was perhaps not for me to

slow things down, or present problems. After all, I had tried just about everything else with so many other dates that had not worked out.

Clearly I was not an expert.

What could go wrong?

Nothing did.

In fact I realised afterwards that perhaps Agnes had done this many times before - it was clever in that there was just enough time to open up that little bit before sharing the movie - one's expectations, other similar movies, any facts we might know, for instance, about the movie itself.

And then after the show, the chance to dialogue about the movie itself.

I know you might find this difficult to believe, but when I tell you what the title of the next movie is that we shared, you might forgive me for saying that I cannot even remember the title of that first one we saw together.

It could not have been particularly memorable.

I do remember talking about it.

But it was that second movie that really did it.

I know that by now you are wondering how it is that I get myself into such trouble, but I feel determined to be honest and to relate things as they unfolded. I can do no more than simply relate the facts.

Agnes was of average height, with brown hair that came down to her shoulders. The muscles in her neck were pronounced and formed a thick V at her throat.

She had classic bow-heart lips, and I felt that in some ways she looked a little like a 1930's movie star.

I do remember that we went out for coffee afterwards at the local Starbucks, and we both ordered a green tea latte.

"I have a list," said Agnes, after we had chatted about the movie we had just seen. "My top five. My top ten. And sometimes," she said, licking her lips, "I can even remember my top 50."

I remained silent.

"I mean, we all see movies, right?"

I felt she was goading me, and panicked a little at the thought of perhaps having to come up with a list of fifty movies I liked. I found myself wishing I had written down all the movies Gord had mentioned in the sauna.

I told her that I had loved the movie about the ship. And then immediately felt silly because I could not remember its name. Luckily for me Agnes was taking a sip of her latte and just that second or two when the cup was at her red lips rescued me, and I remembered *Titanic*.

She smiled.

I didn't think it scored that well. And feeling the pressure on, I racked my brain for other suitable titles.

I told her I loved Life Is Beautiful probably more than any other movie.

"Oh, God, yes," she exclaimed. "What a movie!"

We smiled at each other.

There was a moment of silence. I had anticipated her becoming more animated about *Life Is Beautiful*, but perhaps she was simply lost in the memory of the story.

I cannot think what came over me, but I said that I had loved *Silence Of The Lambs*.

I can't think why I said that because I had been a little frightened when I did watch it some years before.

But true to nature, when feeling confident and totally relaxed sometimes, ideas come flowing out of me that result in my wondering whether it might be better, in future, to keep my mouth permanently shut.

Perhaps I felt the need to impress her with at least some knowledge, perhaps I felt that revealing some details might warn her as to the gruesome outcomes in the movie itself, but I told her that I had recognized that the opening scene of the man abducting the young girl, and then imprisoning her had come from a John Fowles novel called The Collector.

Agnes did seem impressed. "Really?!" I wonder how that worked? Do you think they stole it or did they pay him?"

I said I had no idea.

"That's the one with the FBI agent - Jody Foster?"

I nodded.

"Funny," she said with a little reserve. "For some reason that movie has always evaded me. Perhaps this is why we were supposed to meet. It might be a good choice to watch together some time."

I shifted in my seat, and for some reason wondered whether one of those mentioned by Gord might not be a better idea.

Was the Universe trying to warn me?

Or was it simply my own newly-found Canadian caution?

I racked my brain again, but the one movie I wanted to remember came up only in the picture of a wedding, and I just could not think of its name.

Agnes and I texted a couple of times that next week. We decided on a date for that Friday evening.

She chose a restaurant that had a movie theme. The walls were decorated with posters from many decades of top movies - many of them I recognized, some I remembered without having seen the poster, and some were entirely new to me.

Old cameras were lined up against the wall above our heads, and the most charming feature of the restaurant was a blank wall with a constantly running selection of black and white silent movies.

Perhaps the sight of those movies jangled my memory because I suddenly remembered the name and offered *Princess Bride* as a better choice, but just as I was mentioning the fact that it came as a recommendation from a friend, she interrupted me.

"Oh, yeah! A great movie! Must have seen it so many times - the kind of movie one can see again, and again."

She stopped, and seemed to look at me with a slightly stern expression so that the V in her neck became more prominent. "But I like your first idea. *Silence Of The Lambs* - I think it's going to be an iconic movie for me."

I picked at my food, feeling that I had probably not been properly prepared for that first meeting, with better options to offer Agnes as a first movie-watching choice.

And so I found myself trying to distract her, and decided to say that I had actually been in a movie. Perhaps after my telling her about it, she might even allow me to suggest we watch that instead.

She seemed interested, and leaned forward to hear about it.

When I began to tell her about it, I realised that the reason I had probably mentioned *Silence Of The Lambs* had been because of Anthony Hopkins.

I had always wanted to be Sean Connery when I was young. But my genes had neglected to give me his features, and I definitely did not seem to have his way with women.

Looking back, I realised that I was probably the antithesis of James Bond - while he seemed to be able to bed women within minutes, my own bedding techniques were mostly all but overshadowed by desperate attempts at simply keeping them calm on my couch without vomiting on me, or causing me pain.

Looking back, I feel that this was probably why, deep down, I had chosen Anthony Hopkins as a movie role model.

I felt that my psychic temperament was more suited to his style.

At least he had the ability to make women feel desperate. After all, in *Remains Of The Day*, he had a woman falling all over him while he seemed incapable of recognising this fact and managed to estrange her with each encounter.

His performance seemed to match that of mine.

But somehow I didn't mind, because when I watched him on screen I felt, secretly, that I almost preferred him to Sean Connery.

And so it was that I began my movie career with an attempt at securing a position as an extra in what was to become, sadly, the last movie that another movie hero of mine made before he passed on: *Night At The Museum III*.

Of course the person I am talking about is Robin Williams.

If there is anyone who looked less like Sean Connery, it was him.

Besides Victor Borge, nobody could make me laugh like Robin Williams, and after I watched his skit on golf I was unable to play for some time.

I told Agnes that my movie career started early one morning around 05:30 with me dressed in a suit and tie for the first time in years, and carrying a large suitcase with two changes of clothing "in case the production crew do not like the outfit you have chosen."

The case of clothing turned out to be unnecessary and resulted in being only a heavy burden for the rest of the day until I finally left the film-set around 17:45 that evening.

I had no idea I was in the group that consisted of over five hundred extras for a theatre scene in downtown Vancouver.

While most fell asleep in the audience after only one small packet of lunch, in the middle of the day, with another four hours of tedious shooting to go, I decided I wanted to be visible on screen.

The scene called for chaos on the stage in the theatre that afternoon, and for the audience to react. The director decided that not everyone should rise, scream and run out at the same time.

He called for those with a birthday in certain

months to stand up. When he did, no one in my row did so. I hesitated for a second and then thought this might be my call to fame, so I stood up identifying myself in a birth month that was not mine, but felt only a brief twitch of guilt at my white lie.

I felt that if Merle could tell one and get away with it, it would be okay for me.

Besides no one in my row had stood up and I was worried the director would stop the proceedings, and demand to shoot the scene over again.

I felt sorry for Robin Williams and the rest of them having to burst through the doors, run down the aisle, onto the stage, over and over again.

I felt my standing up provided a service, even if it meant I could prevent one take.

I moved to the aisle seat where no one was sitting, so I could make a quick exit up the aisle towards the doors, flapping my arms wildly in desperate panic as a result of the drama and violence on the stage before us.

All of this was, naturally, on cue when the director called for action.

We did this over and over, and over; so many times, my arms grew tired and with each successive take I became less enthusiastic about raising them.

Also, because I was near the exit at the back of the theatre, I almost collided with Larry Daley, the museum night-watchman, Teddy Roosevelt, The Hun and Sacajawea each time the doors burst open and they all ran down the aisle towards the stage in order to calm Sir Lancelot down.

After one such exhibit of drama, I sat down wearily

and watched as Robin Williams walked up the aisle.

What does one say to a world class comedian? He looked not only weary himself, but depressed. Of course I knew nothing of his struggle at the time.

I raised my hand to my head, as if in a salute, and said "Mr Williams, why the long face?"

He raised his own hand to his soldier's hat, and simply said, "Thank you, thank you very much," smiling a little at me.

I had wanted, during lunch, to walk over and say how much I had appreciated his work. But we had been warned to leave the stars alone - we were only extras, of course.

I remember feeling how little we know of people, when I heard of his demise. And I realised that even then he must have been struggling personally.

I felt I had been insensitive - had I known of his suffering I might have, if nothing else, touched his arm and offered him thanks, instead of he me.

It made me mindful of how easily we can judge people, without knowing what is going on inside of them.

But you can imagine my excitement when the movie finally came out and I managed to locate it on Netflix.

I sat upright in bed one night, popcorn at the ready, a glass of wine on my bedside table, my television ready. I held my remote, ready to hit the pause button.

The scenes came and went and suddenly, almost without warning there we all were, in the theatre.

At one point I could clearly see Henry, a friend I had

gone to the set with, sitting in the audience.

I waved.

I scanned the back of the theatre for a sighting of me.

No such luck.

But then the violence on stage started and I could see the alarm in the faces of the audience; I felt my cue was imminent. I watched intently, and stopped chewing so as to allow for more intense concentration.

The camera zoomed up the aisle; Robin William, Ben Stiller and the bunch burst through the doors.

People rose in their seats, screamed and ran towards the exit. I held my finger adroitly above the pause-button, waiting to see my tall figure and the flailing of my arms. I was dressed in a blue jacket.

Nothing.

I rewound and played the scene over and over but no matter how closely I crept down my bed towards the television and that tiring, gruelling scene, I simply could not identify myself, or the flailing of my arms.

I told Agnes that my appetite for popcorn disappeared and my glass of wine sat unfinished as I contemplated my acting demise.

It was a luckless end to a very long shoot and a particularly short movie career, even though I did get to say hello to my hero.

I looked down, and when I heard nothing from Agnes, I said I was sorry the story was not more exciting and that I didn't feature enough in the movie itself. I did suggest that it might be fun to watch it together.

After all, she might be able to identify me. She

must have seen the sad look on my own face.

"Of course we can," she said, almost with sympathy. "But I still think that *Silence Of The Lambs*, is what I'd like to share with you the first time around."

I smiled.

I was concerned that Agnes might want to watch it at my home because I had the television at the foot of my bed, as I have mentioned.

I did not think it was a good idea to invite a lady to my house on the first date and show her into my bedroom. Especially with a picture of my Emma on the wall above my headboard.

Luckily Agnes said that if I didn't mind, she would make some snacks and we could watch it at her house.

I was relieved. Friday arrived.

I walked up her driveway with a small cooler bag and a bottle of South African Chardonnay inside. I had taken a chance because we had not discussed wine.

"I know sometimes white wine has an effect on me. You know, some people smoke pot and if they're in a dark mood already, the pot makes it worse. Or fearful. Of course it works the other way around," said Agnes.

I raised my eyebrows as I had no experience with pot and could offer no comment.

"Would you believe it, but I've never had a Chardonnay. I always drink Sauvignon Blanc. So this is a treat!"

I opened it and poured her a glass. And then one for me.

I raised my own and offered her the other. She put

her nose inside.

"Oh, my God, that's so smoky! I know the sulphurs in some white wines set me off. I had very bad dreams one night after drinking a Chenin Blanc. But I don't get a smell of sulphur here at all. It's glorious!"

I smiled and took a sip.

It was, as she said, smoky. And it reminded me of the many cellars on so many wine farms around Cape Town.

"And, sooo buttery!"

I smiled again.

Agnes offered me some pâté on crackers, and some olives.

I told her that I had lived in Somerset West near Cape Town for a while, before Emma and I had emigrated, and an Italian magnate had bought a farm, ripped out all the fruit trees and planted the first olive orchard in the entire area.

Some years later he had shocked the Italian olive fraternity in Italy by entering the Grande Olive competition there, had come first, and when the judges had taken their blindfolds off and discovered a non-Italian had been chosen as the best, it caused huge fracas in the press, with one judge resigning.

"That's typical Italian," said Agnes, laughing. "I have some Greek blood, and know how jealously they guard their heritage too, so I'm not surprised."

We sat outside on her veranda, looking over a park opposite her. It was late in the evening, but the sun was still shining.

Of course, I could not say for sure what was to come, but I might have known that the Universe might throw in some co-incidence at this point.

"Look over there," said Agnes. "I think that's some kind of foreign terrier. Oh my god, it looks just like a sheep!"

And she laughed.

It did look just like a sheep, I told her.

The dog looked almost otherworldly, and the image of a sheep suddenly made me think of Mcgillicuddy.

I told Agnes I could remember a story my father had told me about a sheep during the war in Italy.

Perhaps by this time I looked a little more relaxed, a little less desperate about our choice of movie, and so felt comfortable about telling her a story.

Agnes took another tiny sip of the Chardonnay, settled back and gave me a smile that seemed to indicate she wanted to hear it.

He was a tank commander, I told her, and one of his gunners was an Afrikaans man with the unlikely name of Mcgillicuddy.

Agnes leant forward. "The Afrikaners fought the Boer War against the English, right?" said Agnes.

I nodded and said that was why it was strange for one to have such a British name, and apparently also not be able to speak a word of English.

Anyway, I told her, he had the misfortune of having a very bad stammer. In fact there were very few words, besides his name, that he could get out without a severe stutter that left people blushing, and him cringing with embarrassment.

My father had taken him under his wing, and his position as a gunner in the tank was perfect as he didn't have to say much. He proved to be great, and my father said that he had saved their lives a number of times.

It was towards the end of the war, when my father's division was responsible for pushing the Germans north of Florence.

There was some situation in a small town where the Allies controlled one end, and the Germans the other. I told Agnes that I seemed to remember there was a bridge involved, but I shook my head and said that perhaps not, as I couldn't imagine Allied and German troops on either end of a bridge looking at one another.

Mcgillicuddy had managed to capture a sheep. Whether it was on the same bridge or not, or whether it was simply from one end of the town to the other I could not remember, I told her, but when he tried to gain access with the sheep two Allied soldiers, at their end, confiscated it.

Mcgillicuddy had come back to the tank, upset, but not fully able to say why. But the situation became complicated, because those soldiers saw an opportunity, and sold the sheep to some poor civilian entering the town.

Mcgillicuddy, and my father watched as the sheep walked across the bridge with its new owner.

At the other end Mcgillicuddy watched aghast, again, when the German soldiers saw an opportunity for themselves, and also confiscated it.

Amazingly, after some time, the sheep arrived back at the Allied position.

Mcgillicuddy watched this process a couple of

times, and then lost it.

Agnes was laughing. She took another sip of wine.

My father said that when the Germans confiscated it once again, on the other side of the town, Mcgillicuddy had stormed across the bridge, his hand up in the air, approaching them.

Agnes drew her breath in.

They must have been too busy confiscating it again in order to sell it to someone else, because my father said the German soldiers noticed him only when he was upon them.

Apparently he shouted at them so loudly, even my father could hear at the other end.

"Los my fokken skaap. Dis myne. Ek vat hom!" Leave my f#%ing sheep. It's mine. I am taking him!

But my father said, the most amazing thing was not only did Mcgillicuddy say all of this without a single stammer, but the German soldiers simply handed the sheep over to him without a word.

My father always said he was sorry he did not have a camera to take a picture of his gunner walking back across the bridge with that sheep.

Eventually the Germans pulled back, and my father's crew were held up at some manor house where they lived for some months before boarding a ship back to Cape Town.

Mcgillicuddy grew so fond of that sheep, and was never able to slaughter it. He refused, each time, handsome offers of money or contraband.

They spent all their time together, even though Mcgillicuddy had given it the simple name of *Skaap*.

But, I remembered my father saying that what was

truly amazing was that he spoke flawlessly whenever he was with that sheep.

Not one stutter or stammer.

Agnes laughed.

And then for a while we sat in silence, I thinking of Mcgillicuddy and his sheep and Agnes perhaps looking forward to the movie itself.

I followed her inside, and we settled down on the couch. I was careful not to sit too close to her. It was, after all the first real date.

She sat next to me, tucking her feet under a cushion next to her. She leaned towards me slightly.

I made sure that I did not offer anything, like a hand, or even a finger. For just a moment I tried to think what James Bond might do at this point, but then realised that this was silly - he would at least have waited for the movie to start.

It did.

There was Clarice running in the forest. I took a sip of wine, and before I knew it, she was walking down the hallway to the cells beneath in the jail.

I sensed Agnes stiffen slightly.

"Good morning. Dr Lecter, my name is Clarice Starling. May I speak with you?" said Jody Foster.

Agnes stiffened even more when she caught sight of Anthony Hopkins standing so erect in his cell.

I could sense her hand coming across her folded legs. And then it touched mine.

Agnes seemed to relax a little when away from that cell, but when we returned, I could feel her body pulling taut again.

"You use Evyan skin cream. And sometimes you

wear L'Air du Temps," said Anthony Hopkins. And then he looked straight at her and said, "but not today."

Agnes went rigid. "He knows everything about her; everything."

She sucked her breath in and grabbed hold of my hand.

I could feel the sweat from her palms. I wondered what hand cream she used, and whether it would make her sweat even more.

It is funny what comes to mind in a tense situation, I thought.

When Clarice mentioned the ranch in Montana some scenes later, Agnes sucked her breath in even more swiftly than before.

"I went to live with my mother's cousin and her husband in Montana. They had a ranch."

"Was it a cattle ranch?"

"Sheep and horses," said Jody Foster.

I wondered whether Agnes had been to Montana.

I desperately wanted to turn my head and look at her. Perhaps offer her sympathy. But I could not bring myself to do so. I was becoming tense myself.

I said I felt it was perhaps time for a break, and said I was going to the washroom.

"Yes, yes," said Agnes. "I'll, I'll get some more wine."

We both rose from the couch.

She, breathless. I feeling a little weak, also.

We were not even close to the gruelling action scenes. I felt quite desperate about the fact that we were not rather watching *Princess Bride*.

It was much more of a cuddling movie.

I could not imagine Agnes wanting to cuddle with anyone except her mother, once things really got going with the one we were watching.

Perhaps I should go back into the kitchen and tell her I was feeling ill and needed to go home, I thought to myself. But then I realised she would be alone. I could not do that.

I found myself washing my hands and for some reason I could see clearly, in the mirror, a long row of sheep.

I sighed. Lambs, sheep. Why had I even considered this movie, I asked myself shaking my head.

And suddenly I could not rid myself of a memory of the stadium in Bisho, Ciskei, so many years before.

A dark chuckle gave me some relief from the tension when I imagined telling Agnes about the stadium and what had happened there.

But, of course, I realised, I could never do that. Not after the mention of those lambs.

I stared into the mirror, feeling helpless.

Emma and I had moved to a small city called East London on the east coast of South Africa. I had secured a job in the education department at the Presidency of the bantustan called Ciskei which was a fledgling independent state.

Of course, with me being married to a non-white, we did not often feel comfortable in South Africa itself. But the homeland states, of course, welcomed us. It had been a precursor to coming to Canada, and although we did not know it then, Canada would remind us of our time there in that small homeland that seemed to welcome us both with open arms.

But that day, there had been something else. And talk of the sheep ranch had reminded me of this.

I was partly responsible for environmental education in the schools, a mandate that was overseen also by the Department Of Agriculture and Forestry.

They were having their annual Xmas party. They had decided to have it in the stadium in Bisho, the capital. All heads of departments would be there, as well as some cabinet ministers.

Emma had arrived early, and we sat in the hot sun for a short while, until we became too hot.

"You need to come work for us also," said my head of department, Jabulani Sebe, when he shook Emma's hand.

"I'll work for anyone who pays well," said Emma smiling broadly.

"We must make a plan...," said Jabulani, and they both laughed. It was a conversation they seemed to have each time they met, and it always made me smile too.

We sat close to a stone wall for coolth and looked out onto the field below us.

"I wonder when they're going to start cooking," said Emma.

I shrugged my shoulders and said something about Africa-time, which meant that there was never much of a rush.

About an hour later a truck arrived.

Men offloaded three forty-four gallons drums that had been sawn in half, and which made excellent braais, or barbeques. Into that they threw heaps of wood, and then someone poured what must have been paraffin, from a white bottle, onto the wood.

One match, and those three barrels lit up like the afterburner of some rocket.

Emma was startled and leant back in her chair suddenly.

The tables were laden with snacks and other drinks. Some salads and a large container of potatoes.

"I wonder where the meat is," said Emma.

I shook my head. The fires were still burning furiously.

We began to talk about the children back home and what arrangements she had made for them after school.

East London was some sixty kilometres away, and we would probably not be home before the end of the school day.

Some time later, while we sat feeling a little hungry - it must have been well after 1 pm, another large truck arrived.

It reversed into the stadium.

A man dressed in a forestry uniform jumped out and lowered the back. He placed a ramp from the truck onto the stadium grass.

Emma prodded my side, and then looked at me quizzically. I watched carefully.

Out of the truck, and down that ramp, some five sheep were hastened.

At first nothing happened inside of us, Emma and I.

And then she turned, slowly, to me. And I to her.

And she said, "No. No...!"

I held her hand. That time, for some reason, mine

were sweaty. Deep down, I think I realised what was about to happen.

I looked deep into that mirror in Agnes's bathroom, and remembered why I had stopped relating this story. People had simply not believed me when I did.

That day, close to 1:30 pm in the afternoon, with the sun bearing down on that stadium, they lined up those sheep, and with them bleating loudly, they slaughtered them, right there, on that field of grass, and in front of all those dignitaries.

"Well, if nothing else, at least the mutton will be fresh," Emma had said, getting up and going across the floor to speak with Jabulani again.

I was glad she did. Because after they had skinned them, someone climbed back inside the truck and emerged with two chainsaws.

It did not take long to saw those sheep into portions for the braai fire that seemed to be quite ready for the feast.

I don't think I was ever able to rid myself of the sound of those chainsaws in that stadium that day. And the sound of those sheep while they were slaughtering them.

I dried my hands in the basin, in front of Agnes's mirror, as though now cleansed from those deaths I had witnessed, and returned to find Agnes sipping from a very large glass of Chardonnay.

Jody Foster's character went back to see the doctor.

"And one morning I just ran away," she said to him

about living on the ranch.

"You started at what time?" asked the doctor.

"Early. Still dark." she replied.

"Then something woke you... What was it?" he asked.

Agnes gasped. She put her glass of Chardonnay down on the table in front of us.

"And what did you see, Clarice? What did you see?"

"Lambs. The lambs were screaming...," said Clarice.

"They were slaughtering the spring lambs?" he asked.

Agnes began to whimper.

"I opened the gate to their pen, but they wouldn't run. They just stood there, confused. They wouldn't run."

Jody Foster's character looked straight at Anthony Hopkins, through that thick glass.

It was then that it happened.

I remembered having to comfort Emma when she had heard those chainsaws. But that had been a picnic lunch compared to what came out of Agnes that night.

It might have been the look in Doctor Lechter's eyes through the glass that separated him and Clarice Starling, the FBI agent.

Or the slight, barely noticeable quivering of Jody Foster's lips when she remembered the screaming of those lambs.

I never did find out, but whatever it was it ignited some memory deep inside Agnes, as efficiently as that paraffin set fire to the wood in those three barrels.

I have never found out whether in fact she also

grew up on a farm in Montana. Or perhaps in Manitoba itself, where there are many sheep, but when Agnes began to wail, I knew there was a problem.

I felt this had been all my fault, even though I had tried hard to dissuade her. And had suggested *Princess Bride*, or the movie I had been in.

Agnes began to shudder as well as wail, and then with one almighty scream, she flung herself onto my lap and clung to me.

I held her for a while, and then Hannibal Lechter spoke again: "You still wake up sometimes, don't you? Wake up in the dark," said Lechter without so much of any expression on his face, "and hear the screaming of the lambs?"

That was it for Agnes.

If I had perhaps thought she might be frightened by the kidnapping scene, it was nothing compared to the screaming of those lambs that were clearly echoing inside of her.

She clung to me so tightly, I thought I might suffocate.

"I don't want to hear them! Don't let me hear them!" she groaned at the side of my head.

I turned whiter than I had been when I had come out of my mother, at birth.

I put my one arm around her, and grappled for the remote with the other hand.

I found it and switched the television off. For some reason I had anticipated silence.

But it was not to be.

Agnes' screams were louder than anything on that television set and after a while I was tempted to put it back on for some distraction.

Poor Agnes.

It took me twenty minutes to calm her. The rest of that night I sat at the one end of the couch, my head falling forward every minute or two, while she finally fell asleep at the other end, with the blank television set staring at us, as though it were some gaping hole through which her screaming lambs had finally fled.

I never did drink any Chardonnay after that evening.

And every time I look at a bottle sitting somewhere on a shelf, or on someone's counter all I ever think about is Agnes, and the screaming of those lambs.

So deep inside of her.

12

When War Was Right

I never found out whether Agnes blamed me, or whether she simply felt embarrassed. I did text her to ask how she was. And to apologise if she felt it had been my fault. But after a few weeks I gave up wondering.

I shared some of the details with Gord.

Either his dates with Cynthia were not going well, or he was having trouble with his diet, but he offered no comfort, and even less in support of his theory that movies were a turn-on.

Perhaps he had had his own mishap with a similar movie. I did not ask. Instead, later that day I had a chat with Merle.

"Jislaaik Oom. Jy kies fokken Silence Of The Lambs. Is jy mal?!" Jeez, Oom, you chose SOTL. Are you nuts?!

Merle thought this was very funny and could not stop laughing.

"One thing is for sure. If you see her again, you can't cook her *waterblommetjiebreedie* with lamb!"

She was chuckling so much she could hardly get the words out.

I was tempted to put the phone down because I didn't find Merle's mirth that funny at all. But when I remembered her lamb stew with water flowers we call *waterblommetjies* I decided against it. It was a delicacy the Khoikhoi had taught settlers in the Cape, and Merle's was delicious. I got her to agree she would teach me to cook this dish some time, as I was sure I would not be seeing Agnes again.

I still had red marks on my back from her clutching and clawing at me, and I was sure I was a little deaf in one ear from her screaming into the side of my head.

I took a break for two weeks, hid my profile and walked up and down Marine Drive in White Rock a few times each day to clear my head.

Nothing happened for those two long weeks. Except the trains each day, to remind me of Leila.

And when it comes to this next part of the story, I shake my head when I remember what happened, and I remind myself that oftentimes, when I relate these events I, for fear of being mocked or told that I am exaggerating, leave this part out completely.

After all, even Merle said to me: *"Nou praat jy kak."* Now you're talking nonsense.

I didn't even contemplate mentioning this next episode to Gord. I felt that what with his troubles with Cynthia, his diet and his son, I would stand no chance of getting any more advice or support if I told him actually what happened.

Believe it or not Agnes returned, and asked me if I would please share *Full Metal Jacket* with her.

I was so grateful that when she asked me I had not taken a sip of anything, otherwise I was sure it might have come straight out through my nose, just like the Earl Grey tea at the French restaurant with Judy that day.

My immediate reaction was to take a cruise, and text her from the observation deck that I was going to sea indefinitely.

Perhaps even the Arctic.

But Agnes sounded so mournful, and so apologetic that I felt I could simply not avoid seeing her again.

However, I determined that under no circumstances would we watch *Full Metal Jacket*.

I would devise a plan to avoid the viewing.

If the bleating of a few lambs had initiated such a dark quagmire of grief, I was in no way looking forward to being a spectator of her witnessing the butchery of real men in real wartime situations.

I had experienced the reality of this myself. And I didn't think I had any desire to relive such an experience on screen.

Least of all with Agnes.

Apart from anything else I still had some faint marks on my neck.

"I really am sorry," she said to me. "I didn't grow up in Manitoba. But I grew up in Medicine Hat, on a farm. When I was very little, perhaps too little, my father caught me spying on them slaughtering an animal."

I had conceded to meet her again.

This time, we sat on the deck of my White Rock home, looking out over the bay, the yachts and the green Semiahmoo Peninsula of Washington state.

At least it was a view far removed from farms and animals. And definitely from lambs.

I shook my head slowly as I sipped a fresh glass of the wine Agnes had brought.

It was not Chardonnay.

I imagined adding lambs to the long list of aspects of women to look out for and avoid - what with cars, small dogs, large dogs, legal questioning, a penchant for chillies and then multiple allergies the list itself was getting so long I could not fit it under my fridge magnet of Table Mountain.

"He was not cruel to me in any way, but he was very strict. European heritage, you know. Very Protestant, from Denmark."

I nodded. I understood.

"He told me that to be part of a farm was not to just eat the produce, but to also be aware of where it came from."

I coughed, more out of uneasiness than from a need to clear my throat or lungs.

"He called me out of the shadows of the barn, and made me hold the knife. And he made me...."

I immediately rose from my deckchair and told her to stop.

And then I felt ashamed.

It was her story, not mine.

"I know, I know. It's okay. I am sorry. I just wanted to tell you where I was coming from. I am really sorry - we should never have watched that movie, and I know you tried to warn me. I thought I had a handle on things, and stupidly I didn't think that the title necessarily actually meant real lambs."

Foolishly I had not attended to the streaming of the music I played most of the day, and at that particular moment Suo Gan from *Empire Of The Sun* was playing.

And there on my deck I faltered, so that Agnes had to stand up, and put her one hand on my arm. And touching me was, right there, one of the most tender moments I had experienced for a long time.

I was angry with myself because I usually allowed that song to play when I needed to be inspired or moved, and there were few occasions I did not cry when listening to that girl's voice.

I shook my head because I felt so foolish.

I suggested that we set aside any talk of animals, and slaughter. That we simply enjoy our wine and look our across the water.

Agnes agreed.

And after some time of quiet, comfortable silence between us I felt I had devised a plan. I decided I would share my own experience, and in this way convince her that watching a brutal war movie was not the right choice.

I told her that my father had been a rear-admiral and had wanted me to join the navy and become an officer. I had refused.

"Why?"

I took a deep breath and remembered how indignant I had been as a teenager. I told Agnes that I knew all the senior officers in the navy, and felt it was so much a part of my childhood and my personal life that I could not contemplate having it become my full working life also.

Agnes nodded. "I think I understand. Our farm was a part of my childhood too, but when I had a chance to marry a farmer I said no."

I nodded.

I told her that instead I had opted to not have my father pull any strings, and to take my chances with my conscription. My call-up papers arrived and I found myself, just a few months after I had turned seventeen, fighting a war.

"A war?"

I found some relief in first telling her about the Cuban I had met at Granville Island Market in Vancouver. I had picked up some home made sauce in a bottle from one of the tables and he had approached me to tell me about the sauces he made.

He told me he recognised my accent. That it was South African. I tried to think where he came from.

Cuba, he said.

I grew a little nervous.

We fought a war against you and apartheid, he had said to me.

I smiled at him, demurely, I told Agnes.

Yes, he had said. We helped end apartheid.

I was not going to argue with him at all, but knew that the South African troops had suffered few losses compared to the Cubans in their proxy war on behalf of the Soviets. My memory was that it had little to do with apartheid, and more about Russia's stated aim to infiltrate Africa.

It was a long story, I told Agnes, that involved politics and I didn't want to get into it.

"That's okay," she said. "But you said you were there?"

I was, I told her.

"Do you want to tell me about it?"

I pictured her on the couch after the screaming of those lambs had died down, and realised that the only reason I was thinking of telling her about my experience was because I desperately wanted to avoid another episode.

We left immediately after basic training, I said. I had a buddy assigned to me, and me to him. His name was Simon. He was an infantryman like me, but didn't really like guns. At first I had felt a little helpless and wondered why the Universe had put me with him.

But to be honest, I told Agnes, we made a pretty good team. He had a sharp eye, and an acute sense of hearing, and I think he saved our lives a couple of times.

It was a hard war, in the African bush. Hot, dry.

The enemy consisted not only of Cubans but the rebel army from Angola also. We never knew who we might come across in the bush. To be honest, I told her, it was mostly the rebel army. The Cubans were not too keen to engage with us as they knew we had superior fighting skills and experience.

One day we were ambushed. I said it was more just like an attack, although it felt like an ambush.

It was late afternoon and we were dog-tired, I said.

We had walked nearly ten kilometres. Instead of returning to our tents at the base camp, Simon and I went and sat on the edge of the dry river bank, some distance away, under a Mopane tree whose spreading leaves provided a thick and wide roof above us. Taking a cue from the locals, I picked out a small twig and used it as a toothbrush, cleaning between each tooth, feeling the stress of the day and the incessant heat slowly dissipating.

We each had beers. They were cold, ice cold.

I always wondered how they managed to keep only the beers that cold.

I drew on my cigarette, thinking of the day: the walk, the endless vigilance.

No contact, no firing, no enemy.

It had been a good day because of this, but with most of us and our youthful eagerness, and our wanting to go home with having done something, most of us wanted kills.

I was embarrassed telling Agnes this, but it was true. Most of us wanted to have contact with the enemy. It gave us a justified reason for being there, even though most of us hated fighting for the apartheid government itself.

Yet, at the same time, it was a good day because there had been no killing. It was the dichotomy of war.

I remembered each detail so well, I told Agnes.

Simon fumbled in his pocket and retrieved a cigarette himself but did not light it. Instead he pulled the fresh Texan across his upper lip, and drew in the aroma deeply.

I could see a little more of the smiling Simon return. The Simon I had first met in training, in the stark semi-desert far away from where we were fighting the war.

Simon had seemed keen, glad to be alive.

But there in Angola where he had discovered he didn't want to be, he hovered like a coming storm around a dark cloud.

I told Agnes that I tried to lift his spirits, but there was this thing about the war, about fighting, about the few deaths we had seen. It certainly had affected me, I said, but more so Simon who seemed to wither each time we did have a contact. Each time a mortar bomb flew over our heads.

I couldn't make out what it was that troubled him so much more than the rest of us.

Simon threw his head back and let his second beer flow down his throat until the can was empty; he crushed it with his one hand and, belching loudly, he threw it at the toe of his boot.

We said nothing.

It grew dark, slowly, quietly.

The stench that always lies embedded in the heat - the dust. The smell of ancient Africa everywhere, like the smell of a thousand fires. Death. Yet also birth, if birth can smell of something. Dry bush, rocks burning in the sun; bodies drenched in sweat, sometimes blood. The smell of the latrines. All this seemed to slowly retreat as if it too sought some refuge, as the coolness of the evening came to take its place.

Someone lit a fire. I could see it in the dark. Our food was ready. I knew that if I waited long enough someone would bring us some.

Simon said something about some song, his head up against the bark of the Mopane. I laughed at his quirky take on religion.

"Did you know Jesus was a revolutionary, that he liberated women and children?" he asked me.

I nodded.

I remembered the story of Christ sitting chatting to a woman, alone and how bizarre this was, the minister had said, for a Jewish Rabbi to do this.

And I remember thinking, under that Mopane tree, it was a real pity he couldn't come and sit with us there.

I remember, too, asking Simon to sing us a song.

So Simon sang a song about Esther, and her love for Jehovah, and it was to the tune of Nights in White Satin.

I took a sip of wine and told Agnes that only Simon could do that - put some Biblical character into a modern song.

I told her I remembered so well, sitting there feeling content. Each of us with a Texan Plain, and the strong aroma of the fresh tobacco wafting gently up into our nostrils.

But then I felt there was something else, I told her.

Like the thin lines of static in the air just before a quake. Like the smell of a cool breeze just before a cloud burst.

I could sense something coming even though I didn't know what it was.

I took another sip of wine, and looked out at the peaceful scene of the boats in the bay below us. I told Agnes that it was while Simon was singing that it hit us, coming out of nowhere. Nowhere.

We had spent two days pushing the enemy back,

and I was convinced the area had been cleared, but here was the unmistakeable sound of mortars.

Out of nowhere: foefff...whump! foefff...whump!

I felt embarrassed, trying my best to recall what they sounded like, and looked away from Agnes.

She shifted in her seat.

And then the automatic fire, I told her, crackle-popping like dry wood suddenly catching alight. Crackling so loudly.

Tracers were coming across the empty river bed from behind us. Red flashing lights like gigantic firecrackers shot straight up, sput-sput-sputtering their anger.

I watched as some of them seemed to veer upwards at a sharp angle, off course. They looked almost pretty in the evening light.

Then the thumping of some 40mm guns got so loud, I remembered shouting out.

Simon stared at me blankly.

I got up, threw my cigarette down, and ran. This way and that, not knowing what to do. We were far from our tent, with only our rifles. I ran to the nearest bush, then back to the tree, realising how stupid it was to raise my body above the ground.

I must have simply panicked.

There was shouting and then wailing, and the sound of explosions, all around us, mostly on the other side where the camp was.

When I looked at Simon, he looked as though he has been caught stealing something. He looked sad, stupefied, apologetic sitting there up against the tree.

I hugged the ground at the base of the tree, and

watched as Simon turned his body to his left, as if to look behind him. The ground seemed to shake beneath us, and I wanted to move. But where to?

I suppose I felt that if we stayed put nothing would happen to us. But when I looked up and across to our compound, I realised the guys were in trouble. There were bodies everywhere, and they were battling to get to their weapons, get some mortars.

I was sure they didn't even know where the fire was all coming from.

I stopped, gathering myself. Agnes didn't move a muscle.

I continued.

I lay there, staring up at Simon, who seemed to want to turn around to look behind him, as I said.

I reached out to him, and told him not to. "Don't look, Simon! Don't!" I remember saying.

I could hear our captain shouting in the distance. I wanted to stand up and shout back, or run to him, but the tracers scared me.

They were so fast, and they were coming over our heads but missing the tree each time, I told Agnes.

I told her that I could remember seeing them in training, one night, and they had looked like fireflies shooting out into the dark. But now they were more like orange flames, coming at us.

I lay there, expecting to hear one hitting the tree. Would it make a thudding sound, or would it explode? It was so silly, but that's all I could think of.

This went on for…, I wasn't sure. Time was difficult to judge in a situation like that, I told her.

Eventually I couldn't hear any more shouting from

our side. I thought to myself, maybe they're all dead, and here I was pinned down, far away from the camp. What if they found us there alone? But then perhaps it would be our salvation, I remembered thinking. And then I wondered what would happen if everyone was killed and we were left alive, and they came and tortured us.

I can remember thinking that so clearly, like a coward, you know? What kind of soldier was I? I mean, I hadn't done anything besides hug the ground.

Agnes touched my arm.

For a moment I faltered, then I found the strength and continued.

Something exploded inside of me, I don't know what it was. And I stood up.

Agnes waited, then said: "You stood up? Why?"

I don't know, I told her.

I just stood straight up. There seemed to be a lull in the firing and the rate of explosions dropped, so that I could even hear someone crying in the distance, sobbing.

I stood up, and walked away from Simon, leaving him there at the foot of the tree. Then I heard a few mortars again, and once again the crackle of automatic fire. Right there, right then, I just decided I'd had enough.

"So what did you do?" Agnes leaned forward.

I was a little reluctant to continue, but then I did.

I told her I felt silly, and said I didn't know if she would believe me, but I walked towards the firing, onto the verge of the river bank.

There was small dry bush around me, no more than

six inches high. I remember that because I kept brushing against them in the dark. I remember I raised my hands into the air.

And I started shouting in... I paused. I started shouting, I told her.

Agnes stared at me. "Shouting? What did you say?"

I looked at her, as though stupefied: I don't know... I don't know what I said. I found myself talking in tongues.

"In tongues. Tongues?"

Yes. I called out, incessantly. In tongues. All I could think of was Simon behind me, and I wanted it all to stop. I felt out of my depth, far from the camp. My rifle was useless, so I let it fall to the ground. I felt that all I had was my madness.

I used my madness.

I shouted out to them in tongues, I told her.

"Are you sure you don't know what you said?"

Yes. I never spoke in tongues. I learnt it in the Assemblies of God in Kenilworth, but never spoke it in church. I always felt people were crazy when they did. I used to sing and chant it sometimes, as a joke, you know. Just as a joke, sometimes to my friends. But here on the river bank I was shouting it out aloud.

"What happened?" asked Agnes.

I looked up at her. We were both leaning forward, so our faces were that much closer.

What happened?

You won't believe me, I said to her.

They stopped.

They stopped firing suddenly.

Just the sound of them retreating, two or three

vehicles, I think I remember, and the distant sound of an African tongue in the bush. That was all.

Agnes stared at me.

Afterwards Bakkies Oosthuizen, my captain told me he had had word from Command. They said someone had told the enemy to retreat immediately because they would soon be surrounded.

"Did you not perhaps know a bit of their language? asked Agnes. "Didn't you pick up something there, in the bush?"

I shook my head:

No, I told her. I didn't know any other language. I was speaking in tongues, that much I know. What they heard was their business. All I know is they retreated into the bush and left us alone.

Agnes gasped.

I told you it was crazy. Now you can see why I don't talk about this, I said. Never even told my kids. Am sure they would think I was nuts.

"I don't know. I think you should tell them: you're their father," said Agnes eventually.

I was silent for what seemed like a long time, while Agnes shifted in her chair.

I continued. I had to face Simon's father later that month.

"Simon's father?"

I nodded. I told her Simon's mother was dead.

I took a deep breath.

When I went back to the tree, I told her, Simon was screaming. He had taken a shot, or shrapnel in his stomach.

I had my eyes closed when I said this. Then I

opened them and sat bolt upright in my chair.

He was screaming, I said. It was terrible. I fell to the ground, at his side. André, a friend of ours from basic training came to help. Suddenly he was there, out of nowhere.

I bent over, and Simon looked up, through me. Right through me. Not at me, but straight through me.

I tried to get him to focus on me, but he couldn't. He was looking beyond me. This more than anything else, I remember that day.

I remember being upset. Why didn't he look at me? I practically loved him. What was he looking at, right through me on the other side of me?

I sniffed, and wiped a few tears away.

There...there was smoke coming out of the wound, a gaping hole, the size of my fist.

The tears began to flow down my cheeks, and my voice faltered, so that the words came out in disjointed syllables.

I told Agnes I could see his insides, and...and all the blood, but it had al-already stopped flowing. How's that? I mean no flowing blood. Just smoke, or steam or something. Like it...it was some, some trick on stage, you know?

Simon was crying. And André bent down and tried to hold him, but then he screamed.

I rose out of my chair and stood up on the deck, overlooking the bay. I stumbled.

I told Agnes Simon was crying out for his mother. His dead mother. Just imagine.

He cried over, and over, 'Mommy; I want...I want...I

want my Momm-eeyyy!'

I was sobbing myself now, my hands wrapped around each of my arms, as though trying to hold myself in one piece, like I had wanted to do with Simon when I saw that gaping wound.

Right up till the moment...when, when he died. I felt so alone. So alone when he died.

I knelt down, my head almost touching the deck up there above that beautiful shimmering bay, so that I must have looked as though I was praying, and I sobbed, at first loudly, and then more quietly as the memory worked its way through me.

Agnes was at my side.

I hoped that Simon, just before he had died, had felt the comfort I had tried to give him, just as Agnes gave me that day.

She held me for a long time.

After a while a small bird came and sat on the railing as if to watch the spectacle.

And then suddenly, as though it became aware of the intrusion, it flew away.

It was some time before I fully recovered and I could talk again.

Agnes promised me we would never have to watch a war movie together.

And as we finished our wine, sitting there quietly, we were both left wondering, I think, when war was right.

13

Finding My Angel

I saw no movies with Agnes again. I am sure that my war story had scared her off. She did not text me, and neither did I have the courage to contact her again.

After taking another break for a few weeks, I thought about Merle's advice. It was perhaps time to get back on that horse she had spoken about.

Again.

I had been focussing on too many individual things such as cooking, or cars. And small dogs.

It was time to let some *higher power* take over.

Merle got weepy when she spoke about such things.

In particular when she spoke about her encounter with angels, to *special* people.

I felt that everybody was special to Merle, because if a stranger lingered too long, especially when buying flowers, they would hear the whole story.

Every Friday morning Merle delivered flowers to Mevrou Kok of the *Vrouevereniging* at the Groote Kerk. It was right outside the church, one day, that she was knocked over by a bus.

She always said that lying there on the road, with the flowers scattered all around her, and looking up at the roof of Die Groote Kerk in Adderley Street, she had clearly seen angels.

What is more she had even heard them sing.

"They came to fetch me," she told me one day.

She sometimes became tearful, and I would have to put my hand on her shoulder and get her to sit down.

When she had had one glass of wine, she was often more cheerful about the arrival of those angels.

In fact she would even attempt to sing the hymn she said the angels sang from the roof of the church when they came to fetch her that day.

Each time she sang, it occurred to me that it sounded more like the angels themselves were in need of fetching. And if that was the kind of singing the angels used when they came to fetch people, I would rather try to find some way of living for as long as possible.

I never said this to Merle, and always bowed my head in respect when she was singing.

I must admit it was mostly out of fear that they would appear with Merle's singing, and look *me* straight in the eye.

And with this in mind and the memory of this fateful day, I always make a point of walking down Parliament Street, or St George's Mall rather than past the Groote Kerk whenever I am in Cape Town, just in case.

Luckily for all of us the bus driver, who was the son of Merle's sister's husband's brother, gave Merle the *kiss of life*, and she came back.

"From the brink, from the *brink*!" Merle always said with her voice wavering.

And then she would start singing again.

But it was a little different when Merle had had a second glass of wine. She would then sometimes start *vloeking* - swearing - at Ryan, her distant nephew.

She said that when she woke up, the angels were gone. She was angry that he had saved her because the angels were so beautiful up there, on the roof of the church, against the blue sky, and she was happy they had come to fetch her.

In fact, she said, she was sure that it was Ryan's bad breath that had chased the angels away.

"Your turn will come," Merle always said to me. But I never really knew if that meant having to be careful of angels descending from the sky, or whether she meant something else.

I always wondered what might happen if Merle drank more than two glasses of wine, but she never did.

Now, back in White Rock, I felt I had recovered enough, and that I should make another attempt at finding someone.

My time in Cape Town had given me more courage, and besides, although I had no intention of bragging about my cooking to any woman, I had watched Merle while I was there. She had even showed me how to cook pasta.

Merle had said the next time we spoke, she would help me cook a paella.

We skyped that Saturday, and with my iPad propped up against the kitchen backsplash, as they call it here in Canada, I asked Merle to teach me something other than Bobotie, or melktert.

She talked me through the paella dish she had promised. I even learnt how to pronounce this Spanish word - *pah/EH/yah*.

Merle remembered that my mother had taught me how to cook rice so many years before and that Tastic rice is still one of my favourites.

We decided on a simple chicken dish, and she showed me how to add a tin of smoked oysters, some capers, and with cumin and turmeric as seasoning.

I had bought a large flat frying pan with sides because Merle had said it could double up for stir-fries, even though it was not technically a wok.

It was simple enough because everything hinged on the rice, and rice was something I understood. Of course, probably because I am a man, I did not follow the recipe exactly. When I found out that saffron could cost more than one thousand dollars a pound, I decided to think of something else.

After taking a hard look at the jar of curried chillies, I made up my mind to leave it exactly where I had put it that day after my encounter with Mrs Paine, and closed the fridge door.

I decided I should try to experiment with something else. So I added some *pimentón ahumado* - I felt that I might be cheating by leaving the saffron out, so

I had bought a tin of this smoked paprika at Granville Island when I noticed it had also been imported from Spain.

The paella was just fine. In fact it was delicious.

Although I did not want to particularly use any recipe, or my ability to cook, in order to find someone, I did feel it gave me a little more confidence.

I went back on to Match.com.

After a few hours I decided to eat another plate of paella. I was getting nowhere, and after finishing my second meal, I went to bed having found no one with promise.

But as I was falling asleep there was a *ping* sound that came from my computer. I had left Match.com open and someone had probably contacted me.

I was too tired to get my head off the pillow, so I ignored it.

The next morning, with a mug of coffee at my side, I sat in front of my computer screen, and there was a new message.

Someone by the name of *jugfulloflove* had favoured me, winked and sent an email: *I liked your profile, especially your African connection; want to try meeting?*

I studied the screen as I sipped my coffee. She was short, with blond hair. Fifty-six. Cute. I could find nothing about Africa in her profile, so was not sure what she had meant.

No dogs.

No kids.

No cars. Not any that I could find amongst the eleven pictures in her profile.

But then I reminded myself I was not supposed to focus on such things, because I didn't want it to be like listening to Merle, and worrying about the angels coming.

I had promised myself I would let go. So I didn't look specifically for cars, or dogs.

But I kept a small eye open, just in case.

I felt she was worth a meeting. Besides she had contacted me first.

I emailed back and said I thought that would be fine.

To my surprise, she replied immediately.

We decided to meet in Vancouver, and whether it was my tempting fate or just being brave, I suggested Mahony & Son's on the water.

Again.

After two fateful meetings there, I wondered whether I was not perhaps taunting Merle's angels. Or mine.

But the setting is spectacular, overlooking the Creek with the yachts, the water taxis and people enjoying the water. And the beer is good.

I decided to take my time and drive there before the appointed 5:30. This was in order to find parking and settle myself down upstairs, on the deck. Nice and early.

I looked at her picture again. She had signed off her email to me with *Jess*. I could not think of any Jess in my past, so there was no story to mull over.

But sitting there, with my mind wandering, and with the taste of the coffee in my mouth, I thought of Merle again.

And how she fluctuated between *vloeking* when speaking about her distant nephew, Ryan, who had had bad breath, when he chased the angels away, and the fact that she was grateful to him for saving her life. Every now and then, when she was talking about being saved *from the brink*, she would seem grateful and say that had it been another driver, he might not have given her that kiss of life.

And she might have died.

She said that it was a co-incidence that Ryan, her distant nephew, had been the one to knock her over in the first place.

But then it seemed that when the wine had settled down comfortably inside her, she would offer more wisdom, because when she drank white Chardonnay - and it is strange, but it was always the Chardonnay that brought this about, she would lean forward, focus her eyes on me, and say that there was no such thing as co-incidence.

That if something happened, it was meant to happen.

That if someone showed up in one's life, they were meant to be there.

I often thought about this because I had heard of a few co-incidences, and even experienced a few myself.

Like when Emma and I moved to Vancouver to get away from our difficulties in South Africa, we lived next door to Sharon, the daughter of the Jewish vet from Simon's Town - the naval town just south of Cape Town itself.

When I had moved there as a child, my mother and

father had dogs and when we needed a vet, it was Doctor Schmidt we always went to.

Imagine, that his daughter and I should meet up for the first time in Vancouver thousands of miles away and in a different hemisphere, and not where we grew up together.

But there are a few others I can remember.

When Uncle Storky retired, he and his wife went on a tour of Europe. In the seventies many people did this. They went to Sweden, bought a Volvo, toured Europe and then the South African government allowed them to bring the car back without duty, if the car was six months old.

It was a big thing in those days, because cars in South Africa have always been expensive. Uncle Storky was so proud of his Volvo. It was burnt orange. In the seventies orange was a very popular colour.

And talking of colour, what an amazing story he told us when they returned.

He and his wife Aunty Bobbie, which was short for Bobbita, were standing in Piccadilly Circus in London. I think they were looking for a theatre or some shop. Of course Uncle Storky must have turned to Aunty Bobbie and said something in Afrikaans.

Suddenly he felt a tap on his shoulder.

He spun around, perhaps worried it might be a thief or a mugger. It was a coloured man, from Cape Town.

"My jerre my baas! Dis lekker om 'n wit man te sien!" *Goodness, boss; it's great to see a white-man!"* he said to Uncle Storky.

Of course, Uncle Storky, the *white man* was the

baas back home. But it took the humour of this man to make light of this, and we laughed every time he told this story. And I remember Uncle Storky shedding one tear whenever he did. It was strange, but it was only one tear every time.

He would wipe it away, and then laugh with all of us.

I am not sure why it was important for Uncle Storky and Aunty Bobbie to meet this Capetonian. At the same time I am also not sure whether it is my job in life to consider such things as deeply as Merle sometimes does, like when she remembers the angels. I decided, long ago, to simply accept what happens to me without asking too many questions.

There was another co-incidence, one day, that I have not forgotten. This one happened to me.

I was sitting at Café Verdi in Wynberg.

I think someone, one day, told me that it is the oldest pub in Cape Town. I like to think this, even though the manager said it was once an art shop. The idea of it always being a pub is more appealing to me because I like beer, and because that part of Wynberg, known as the Chelsea District, was the headquarters of the British Army during the Boer War.

But, of course, that is another story.

I was sitting there with Emma my wife, on one of our visits, before we had emigrated because the apartheid officials wanted to separate us. They said we were being immoral when we got married, even though we loved one another so much.

That was when we came to Canada which did not mind us being coloured and white. In fact I don't think anyone even noticed.

And, of course, that is also another story.

But there we sat - me sipping my beer, and Emma a cocktail with lemon, because she loved lemons.

The owner knew me well, and simply ignored the segregation laws in his restaurant, besides Emma could sometimes pass for being white. Cape Town was like that, and we often found places to be together without making trouble.

We sat at the back, outside, under a large umbrella, with tables and chairs all around us, and the thick bushes of lavender everywhere. When a light breeze blew, the whole place was like a breaking wave - on the shore of our love - we used to say together.

That is the way I remember us, sitting there amongst those purple flowers, like a wave of love coming over us.

We must have been there for quite a while. A young man walked past us, and sat down. I might not have even noticed him, but he arrived with a Dalmatian puppy. It sat quietly next to him under the table.

And I could not help but think of Zsa-Zsa. And while I watched the puppy sitting there so calmly, I told Emma about my mother during the war.

She had finished school in the early forties, and for some reason decided to join up. I think it was the Queen's example. I am sure she saw a picture of her driving the ambulance on Pathé news in the local bioscope.

In those days all guns on the coast were controlled by the Coast Artillery, so her uniform was more army than it was navy. They built a 9.2-inch gun on Robben

Island to protect Table Bay from German u-boats, but I don't think any of them arrived.

Anyway, they didn't know this for sure then, and for some time she served as a plotter, under the gun, in the operations room.

Her own mother, a nurse, came down from Pretoria with her, and they lived in a small one bedroom apartment in Three Anchor Bay while my mother served as proudly as the Queen herself.

The apartment was on a hill, and sometimes my grandmother could not get her 1928 Austin up because the fuel was gravity-fed. So she had to reverse up to where they lived.

In fact she was often seen driving backwards up hills, to see private patients. She was a good nurse and I told Emma how much I missed her because she was the only one who could put a bandage on a finger properly.

It was there, on Robben Island, that my mother met my father. He was first a tank commander up North, and then joined the marines when he came back, and so they put him on the island because of the big gun there.

But that is yet another story.

While my mother was posted there during the war, a friend from Greenpoint asked if she would adopt a Dalmatian that had gone deaf.

Her name was Zsa-Zsa. No doubt the famous socialite and actress had been a favourite with my mother's friend.

Zsa-Zsa had not been able to hear traffic and had taken a tumble when a car hit her.

My mother accepted the commission, and Zsa-Zsa came over on the Robben Island ferry called the Issie, which was named after Field Marshal General Smut's wife and for some years, before Zsa-Zsa died, she lived happily without the threat of motor vehicles.

Everyone on Robben Island would watch out for her - she was easy to notice with her white coat and black spots.

My mother always told us children how she would simply stomp on the wooden floors of the house where they were living to summon her.

I remember we all giggled when she told us this, and my sister and I always stomped on the wooden floors of any house we could find when we remembered her telling us about Zsa-Zsa.

It was as if the Universe had decided that this story was remarkable, because while Emma sat listening to me, I could notice the young man shifting in his chair.

He had been sitting quietly minding his own business, and drinking his beer, but he must have heard some of what I had said because he leaned over and said the most remarkable thing: "Are you talking about Zsa-Zsa, the Dalmatian during the war on Robben Island?"

I looked at him, blankly.

I nodded.

"I read that story in the Naval archives when I was working there. And I decided to buy myself a Dalmatian. Come Zsa-Zsa," he said. "Come here."

The dog got up and came over to greet me.

I stroked her gently, feeling almost as though this was a privilege I did not deserve.

And I remembered what Merle had said about co-incidences, and the fact that they did not exist because things were meant to happen. At times, I have tried to imagine what the meaning of this meeting with Zsa-Zsa was, that day. Perhaps there was some significant connection.

On the other hand, perhaps it was just the Universe smiling at me. And my mother, even though she was not there because her own angels had already come for her.

We chatted for a while and then the young man, and Zsa-Zsa left the pub, and walked down the road towards the magistrate's court.

Emma smiled as we watched him leave.

I remember her reaching out to me, as though she was saying that we had meant to meet, also.

I squeezed her hand, sensing that she was right.

And, now, as I took a slow drive down Highway- 99 towards False Creek in order to meet Jess, I could not help but think of her again and how happy we had been.

Parking can be a problem in any large city, but in Vancouver I sometimes get my signs confused - one saying that parking is free for two hours. But only after or between certain hours.

Down the road another sign will say something quite different. I had had my car towed away one Saturday morning while parked outside a small pre-primary school that was closed. It cost me so much to get the car back, I realised it was enough, in South African Rands, to keep a family alive for a whole month.

I had told Merle on skype, and she had asked why they were so greedy.

Being early meant that I would have time to locate a good parking, and make sure I came back to a car.

I drove down the only road that ends up at False Creek itself, on the south side. The parking sign said I had two hours free, until 6 pm.

I parked.

Just to make absolutely sure, I approached a young man who had arrived with his partner. He looked the intelligent type. Luckily for me he said the 6pm condition meant that after that hour, it was free the whole night, until 8 am the next morning.

I think he might have seen the look on my face, because he said he was sure, and I was not to worry.

I walked the short distance, along the Creek, towards the restaurant and pub.

It was a beautiful day.

Emma and I visited the restaurant often when it was known by another name. I had not wanted to return after she had died, and I had missed sitting on the deck, looking over the water.

When the present owners bought it and opened with a fresh look and a new name, I had felt brave enough to enter again.

Now, I was glad I did. I had agreed to meet Jess upstairs, so we could look down onto the water and the boats.

I entered through the brand new heavy wooden doors.

"Oh, sorry, the upstairs is booked for a private function," said the server at the welcome desk.

I walked to a chair against the bar and sat down.

It made me think of The Paulaner Bräuhaus at the Victoria & Alfred Waterfront in Cape Town, upstairs. If anything, that pub had taught me the value of a setting.

Sitting up there, just before the sun went down, with my Emma, was almost as good as being in the veld overlooking a waterhole, with the animals coming down to drink, and the dust of the African bush making the world look as if the angels had sprinkled gold everywhere.

I could not sit downstairs, I decided; I had to be on the veranda, looking down on the water.

If Merle could rise from the dead, I could find a way, I thought to myself.

I walked up the stairs, with the girl who had given me the sad news of being banned from going, looking askance at me. When I arrived, I looked around. The view through the windows was special - the apartment blocks across the water gleaming. The water taxis. The boats. Some tied up and looking alone. Others occupied, with their owners sitting on their decks, drinking a glass of wine.

It was a place of celebration, and it was what made Vancouver wonderful in summer.

An important-looking man walked past me. I was sure he might be the manager.

I beckoned to him and he turned around.

I asked if the *entire* pub upstairs was booked out. I told him that I was meeting someone.

I think he saw the look in my eye, and knew what I meant, because I could detect a very tiny smile.

At least it was not a wink.

I said that I did not want to meet her downstairs, because the view from up there was what I really wanted.

I felt there was some conflict inside of me, right there, when I told him this. Emma and I had often sat upstairs in the old pub and enjoyed the view from the balcony.

And here I was attempting to meet someone new. Someone I had not even met before.

But then, looking around, not only because everything was brand new, but also because I knew I was better only because of Emma, I felt I could do this.

"Oh, sure," he said. "Inside is booked out for a private function, but out there, on the east deck? You're welcome to sit there and I'll have someone come out to attend to you."

I felt as warm, inside, as an African sunset, and I thanked him.

I found a table. Right on the edge.

I ordered a beer and took out the investment magazine I had brought to keep myself occupied while I waited for Jess.

Looking down across the water and the Creek, at the mountains in the distance, I wondered what Merle might say sitting there next to me. I imagined it would remind her so much of Cape Town.

But then I thought of her angels, and returned to an article on solar energy in the magazine I had brought.

The waitron brought my beer. When I looked up at her, I suddenly realised that I could not leave my table, for fear of losing it, as there were other people arriving.

I felt embarrassed, but said that I was there to meet someone.

She smiled.

I told her that I had said we would meet upstairs, overlooking the water, and that she had agreed. But I was afraid that they would tell her that upstairs was booked up just like they told me.

I said that if I went downstairs, I might lose the table. I asked if she had occasion to pass the entrance now and then, and if she might feel open to looking out for the person I had planned to meet.

She smiled, again.

I was starting to feel uncomfortable, but I smiled back, nevertheless.

I did think she was smiling a bit too much for such a young lady, especially when an older man, like me, spoke of such intrigue.

It was about then that I was sure she winked at me.

I found myself not knowing where to look, and I almost knocked over my beer.

I felt that perhaps I should tell her that I had no bad intentions. And that it was just a meeting.

"Don't worry about it. Just tell me what she looks like, and I'll direct her up here," she said.

I told her Jess was around fifty-five and blond. Average height for a smaller woman. And of slight build.

I felt embarrassed, as I didn't want this to sound like some kind of auction. Like when Uncle Storky spoke about his cattle on the farm in the old Transvaal.

It was then that I think she actually winked at me again.

She left, and I found myself taking a long, deep sip of that cold beer as I looked down onto the water.

I decided that I needed to look cool, as the younger generation said, and consulted my magazine while I adjusted my new pair of spectacles that darkened in bright sunlight, and that now sat on my nose.

I felt embarrassed.

Down on the water there was a yachtsman approaching a buoy. I remembered the last one. This one made it.

His wife secured the buoy, and he reversed the engines just in time. I envied them down there on the water and I got to thinking that perhaps I might buy a boat one day. Having spent part of my childhood in the naval village of Simon's Town, I got to love the sea.

I wondered if choosing a boat was as difficult as finding a female companion.

Suddenly there was a presence on my left. I looked up.

"Hello," said a woman's voice. "Sorry I am a bit late, but had a day at work."

I rose.

Without thinking, I kissed her on the left cheek, feeling relieved that she had finally arrived. She giggled. We both sat back down and I asked her what she would like to drink.

"Oh, do they have cider?"

I said she was lucky as they had not only cider, but had it on tap.

She laughed.

I felt there was something in that laugh of hers. Especially the way her eyes closed when she did so.

The young girl came back, and I ordered a cider for her

It was sunny, it was hot. It was Vancouver at her best.

She spoke a little about coming straight from work, and that she had been afraid she might be late. Her drink arrived.

"Oh, my God, I needed that," said Jess as she lowered her glass.

I told her the whole story of upstairs, downstairs. She leaned over, a little like Merle after some wine, and I elaborated some more.

We both laughed then, together.

Perhaps it was just the beer I had been drinking, that made me feel so comfortable, but I felt there might be something special also, in her.

I asked about her being involved in health care.

"Oh, no. I am with the city. HR."

I smiled, feeling embarrassed. It was the first time I had gotten a profile wrong. I wondered how I could get so confused. Especially since I had not been dating for some time.

"My brother-in-law had the same accent as yours," said Jess. "South African, right?"

I nodded.

For some reason a picture of Andréa came to mind. I wondered whether I should ask if her bother-in-law had *had* his accent, or whether he still *had* it.

She looked over at me. Her hands were small, but

as she lifted her glass, once again, I noticed how beautiful her fingers were.

The scarf that hung around her neck fell down onto the table and sitting there, an African so far from the bush, now in Canada, I felt that perhaps some of Merle's angels were smiling down on me.

I was careful not to look up too high, though, in case I might just meet their gaze.

We chatted about the weather. All Vancouverites seem to talk about the weather in every conversation.

We also talked about how privileged we felt, being there on the water, and with the mountains looking down onto us.

And I told her how it was in Cape Town. Just the same. And then she said she loved to travel and had been on many cruises, but never to South Africa.

And then we fell silent.

I got the feeling that she was as calm and peaceful as I was feeling, right there in the basking sun.

After a few minutes, I felt the need to say something again. Just to liven things up, so to speak.

"So is Jess short for Jessica?" I asked.

There was a tiny breeze, and it lifted her scarf so that it floated sideways against her cheek where I had kissed her. And for some seconds it remained there, quite still, as if waiting for something to happen.

I sensed the Universe was about to say something important. It was as though a little angel had coughed. Or sneezed.

She looked at me.

"Jess?" she said.

I stared at her. And she at me.

It felt like a long time.

"You're.., you're not Jess?" I said slowly, looking at her scarf.

"No," she said. "My name is Ester."

"Ester?"

"Yes. Ester."

And then she took a good look at me.

"You aren't Peter, are you?" she said smiling.

I shook my head.

"They call me Oom," I said.

"Oo-im?" said Ester putting her hands up against her mouth in surprise.

There, we hung in midair, not able to speak. Not able to think.

The woman in front of me, Ester, leant forward and began to laugh.

"Oh, my God!" she said. "Where is Peter?"

Peter? I shrugged my shoulders.

We both looked towards the entrance.

The waitron walked past us, smiled and then went through the veranda doors into the main restaurant.

Ester and I began to laugh, as if the sunshine had touched us after many days of rain. And for some reason we just knew that it would be the first of many laughs together.

And when we talk about it now, and laugh all over again, I often wonder whether she knows what I am thinking inside my head. Whether our meeting was just a co-incidence, or whether a co-incidence could also be a meant-to-be.

Merle had been right - my time *had* come and I

know, now, that instead of the angels coming to fetch me, as they had done with Merle that day the bus ran her over, and before Ryan's bad breath had chased them away, they had come this time to give me someone special. That someone special Mr Solomon himself had spoken about too.

Since our second date I have called Ester my Little Angel.

And she smiles every time I do.

And sometimes I do think our meeting like that was meant to be, because that big hole inside me - the hole that Emma had left when her own angels had come?

It is now gone.

Made in the USA
Columbia, SC
06 August 2017